Jean

Leonora

Leonora

by Catherine Fellows

A FAWCETT CREST BOOK

Fawcett Publications, Inc., Greenwich, Conn.

LEONORA

THIS BOOK CONTAINS THE COMPLETE TEXT
OF THE ORIGINAL HARDCOVER EDITION.

A Fawcett Crest Book reprinted by arrangement with
Hurst & Blackett Ltd.

Printed in the United States of America

1

Captain Louis Matheson sat on a fallen tree and reflected that for someone with scruples, his present occupation was singularly ill chosen, and definitely not to his taste when the wind was blowing strongly from the north-east. His big bay horse tugged on the reins, trying to reach a distant clump of grass, and the captain looped them over his arm so that he could thrust his hands into his coat pockets. He sank his chin and ears further into his ample collar, and regarded his horse's black legs with a scowl, informing him with a certain bitterness that he had the most uncomfortable gait of any animal he had ever ridden.

The bay pricked his nose on a holly branch, and the captain grinned, and relaxed against the tree until his ready ears caught the rumble of a carriage, and the quick clop of hoofs. Immediately, he mounted and pressed the bay nearer to the edge of the road.

A rider appeared round the bend, then an antiquated carriage, drawn by what was, in the captain's opinion, a very inadequate pair of horses.

Feeling that this was a poor return for his long wait in the cold, the captain sighed, pushed up his mask, loosened his pistols, and rode calmly into the centre of the road, casually firing over the heads of the coachman and groom as he did so. He then trained his second pistol unwaveringly on the centre button of the escort's coat, and with exquisite politeness requested their weapons.

The coachman yielded up his blunderbuss with a pleasing promptness, but the rider, due to the wild plunging of his high-bred mount, was fully occupied for some moments in the vital business of keeping his seat. With a flicker of amusement, the captain recognised him as Sir Mark Finchley, and watched the equestrian display with increased appreciation.

'If you would be good enough to drop your weapons,' he repeated gently. 'I thank you. Now over there.' He indicated the side of the road with a wave of his pistol, and after a slight hesitation the groom climbed down and joined Sir Mark. Keeping a wary eye on the roadside, the captain backed towards the coach and opened the door.

A shriek rent the air immediately, and he reflected that his first instinct, which was to let the coach go by, had been well founded. An ill-matched pair and an aged equipage had held little promise at the outset, and robbing ladies was against the captain's principles. He closed the door hastily, bowed, and was about to depart when the window was let down with a snap, and the muffled shrieks suddenly rang out clearly in the night air.

Against this background a face appeared, illuminated by the bright moonlight, dark ringlets danced indignantly, and an icy voice informed the captain that its owner had nothing of value, unless he fancied her paltry garnet earrings, or a bunch of artificial flowers, and that she desired nothing so much as her bed.

Intrigued, the captain sat his horse and smiled down at her, waiting for the indignant spate to end.

'Madam,' he said eventually, 'if it had not been a particularly unsuccessful evening, I would offer to make up your deficiencies of adornment. As things are, I can only offer you my sympathies and apologies.'

He grinned again, as there was an affronted gasp from the coach, and was once more about to depart when his horse, most agreeable where humans were concerned, but unreliable with his own kind, aimed a kick at the nearest carriage horse.

The captain slapped the bay good-humouredly across the quarters, but his hat was jerked to one side. In the second before he straightened it, a distinctive silver streak was revealed in his otherwise dark locks.

Detecting a shade of amusement in the face that watched him from the window, he lingered by the coach. It was not his practice to dally while on business, but then never before had his appearance on the scene provoked such reaction in a prospective victim. Under his regard she flushed, and withdrew from the window, and, regretfully, the captain was just about to wave the groom back to his seat when he was arrested by her urgent whisper. 'Quickly! The pistols! By the roadside!'

Mentally cursing, the captain remembered that he had left them uncollected, and whirled his horse. Sir Mark, down on one knee, was just lining him up in the sights, and, bending low, the captain thrust his heels into the bay's sides and made for the trees. He had almost reached cover when a shot rang out and he felt a burning pain below his left shoulder, and heard thudding hoofs in pursuit. He urged the bay on, and the big horse lengthened his stride, wheeling and turning in the uncertain light, as the captain, from necessity riding one-handed, neck-reined him through the trees.

The hoof-beats died away behind them, and with relief the captain pulled him to a walk and rubbed his mane affectionately.

'Caesar,' he regarded the mobile ears with satisfaction, 'I hold by what I said concerning your paces, but I forgive you because you are the fastest and most obliging beast I have ever ridden.' He felt his arm tentatively. 'And don't ever be tempted to linger over a pretty face,' he added.

Wriggling his fingers, he discovered they were sticky, and not liking the thought of so much of his good blood being wasted, he abandoned all thought of making his original destination and kept on through the woods.

He skirted the village whose lights showed faintly through the trees, and remarking conversationally to Caesar that he hoped there were no rabbit holes, followed the road on the other side of the hedge, until, just after the last cluster of cottages, he came to an inn.

Instead of being decently deserted, the yard was full of vehicles and scurrying ostlers, and, sighing faintly, the captain fumbled his way round the back and stabled the bay himself. He felt himself unequal to the task of rubbing him down, and, instead, stuffed some straw under an old horse blanket and hoped fervently that he would dry off before he took cold.

Carefully scuffing the drips of blood as he went, he retreated towards the door and let himself out into the darkness. The moon had disappeared, and after falling over a pitchfork, he stood for a moment while his eyes readjusted, reflecting that it could just as easily have been a bucket, in which case the resultant clatter would certainly have brought someone out. Making his way round the outbuildings to the inn, he narrowly escaped disaster crossing the yard, but a muffled cluck held him in his tracks.

Peering closely, he was able to make out rows upon rows of hens roosting on poles under an open shed. Muttering savagely that the landlord well deserved to have them taken by foxes, he retraced his steps to come to the back door by another route. Quietly letting himself in, he slid past the kitchens, and ducked hurriedly under the dim stairway as footsteps sounded at the far end of the passage. From his dark recess he saw it was the landlord, and relaxed, suddenly aware of his tensed neck muscles. He gave a gentle whistle, and the landlord spun round.

'Party of gentlemen in the front,' he explained briefly, thrusting the captain into a back parlour. His eyes took in the bloodstained fingers, and widened. 'Lordy, sir—you're hurt!'

'Curb this unseemly habit of yours, Joe, of addressing highwaymen as "Sir",' the captain said reprovingly. He peeled off his coat and rolled up the shirt sleeve to examine the results of Sir Mark's parting shot. As he thought, it had hardly more than nicked the flesh, and though it bled freely, the actual damage was slight.

'Not but what the next one might be through your heart,' Joe said, as he ministered to it. 'Fine way for a gentleman to be carrying on. Someone is going to recognise you one of these fine days.' He gave a sharp tug to the last knot of the bandage, and the captain winced.

'Peace, my friend. I have this very evening decided to abandon it as a career. Others are adopting my style and dress, and Black Gentlemen are springing up all over the country. I am robbed of my distinction. Besides,' he added, 'it's getting too damned cold to be hanging about in woods playing Robin Hood. I must be getting nervous too. Those hens of yours gave me a scare. Why the foxes haven't had 'em all I can't think.'

'Nervous!' Joe scoffed. 'After trailing the length and breadth of France under the noses of Boney's agents! Nervous of a few hens!' He got up to throw the blood-stained cloths on to the fire, and poured out a couple of measures of brandy. 'Anyway, the old dog would smell out a fox a mile away.'

'Well thank God his nose isn't as good for highway-men,' the captain said, sipping his brandy. 'He didn't smell me when I came through the yard. By the way, I wasn't able to rub Caesar down. I've put him in the far stable. Give him an extra measure of corn. He left that thorough-bred mare of Mark Finchley's standing, bless his Roman nose.'

'Mark Finchley,' Joe groaned. 'As well hold up your own mother!' He found he was clutching the neck of the bottle, and absently refilled his glass.

'I didn't hold him up. He was escorting the coach I held up.' He raised an enquiring eyebrow. 'Old carriage— looked like a pair of work-horses—dark-haired girl about nineteen, twenty?'

Joe shook his head. 'No. Finchley's place is about fif-teen miles from here. No call for him to come this way.' He became aware that the captain was staring pointedly into his empty glass, and hurried to repair the omission. 'I'll nip out to the nag as soon as I've seen supper through to this party in the front, all supposing they haven't boozed themselves under the table. Breaks your heart to put decent food in front of them when they don't know what they're eating!' He stood up and stretched. 'I'd best see to them now.'

The captain nodded. 'I'd like a pen and paper when you come back. It's time I began to set my affairs in order.' He felt his arm tenderly. 'How fortunate that he got me in the left!'

When the landlord, between steaming courses of roast duck, fish, and pies, slid in his requirements, he briskly wrote out and sealed his letter, gave a small smile at the probable reaction of the recipient, and retired, untroubled, to bed.

Back in the coach, Miss Leonora Revell was attempting, with a certain amount of irritation, to soothe her hysterical maid.

'For heaven's sake, Betty, stop your screeching!' she expostulated finally. 'He neither harmed us nor took anything. He'd have had a hard time to find anything worth the taking,' she added bitterly.

Betty cautiously lowered her cloak, which she had flung over her head at the first sight of the frightful figure in the doorway, feeling that whatever fate was about to overtake her, she could better endure it with her eyes covered.

'He might have ravished us!' she said in trembling tones.

'Not if he had seen me in this bonnet and pelisse,' Leonora retorted flatly. 'Besides . . .' She was about to point out the obvious difficulties entailed in keeping three able-bodied men covered with a pistol while he accomplished his fell purpose, but realised it would be indelicate.

She let down the window again, and poked her head through. The coachman and groom were shouting each other down with conflicting versions of their part in the affair. Leonora merely thanked them for their heroic attempts to defend her, and bade them take care that the mettlesome pair in the harness didn't get away with them.

These were standing with their heads hanging down, comfortably resting a hind leg apiece, and as oblivious of the action around them as if they had been back in their stall. She surveyed them with disgust, and turned her attention to the bridle path down which Sir Mark had disappeared in his triumphant pursuit of the highwayman, and whither, in a few moments, he returned, panting and red-faced.

'He got away,' he said breathlessly. 'But I certainly hit him! Are you all right, Miss Revell?'

'Yes,' Leonora said baldly. Feeling that she was probably showing a lamentable want of sensibility, she summoned a flutter to her voice. 'We suffered a severe shock, of course. Highwaymen upon this road! I declare I shall never feel easy along here again! Do you think you have killed him, Sir Mark?'

Sir Mark swelled visibly. (And he could ill afford to, Leonora thought venomously.) 'As to that, I cannot be sure, but we shall see no more of him tonight. I must get you back to your parents, Miss Revell. You will recover more readily from this unhappy affair when you are safely home.'

The rest of the journey was accomplished in silence, Leonora biting the worn tip of her glove as she pursued her own line of thought. Whatever had possessed her to warn the highwayman! He was tall, and sat his horse with grace, but he might be an absolute ruffian under his mask. She remembered then that he had spoken with a cultured accent. In fact, as far as voices went, he was more the gentleman than Sir Mark.

In comparing them, she conjured up the picture of Sir Mark's self-satisfied countenance, which persisted, in spite of her best efforts, in floating before her inner eye. She sighed as the pot-holed road gave way to the drive of Revell House, and clutched the strap in anticipation of the rut which the coachman never missed, even though it had been there three years to her knowledge.

The coach stopped, and she allowed Sir Mark to assist her tenderly up the wide, shallow steps to the front door, which was badly in need of a coat of paint, and was opened by a butler who would similarly have benefited from refurbishing.

Once inside, Betty fled for the servants' hall, eager to impart her tale, and enjoy her role of heroine of the hour, while Leonora and Sir Mark were bowed into the drawing room by the decrepit retainer.

This apartment, even in the candlelight, wore a faded look, the velvet curtains showing pale streaks from long exposure to sunlight, wallpaper darkened by smoke above the candle brackets, and the originally expensive brocade on the chairs, sadly rubbed on the corners.

Lady Constance, a notable needlewoman, had unpicked the spare material from underneath the seats, intending to repair the worst of the splits, but the results of her labours were not satisfactory. She was displaying with horror to Mr. Revell and Maria the difference in colour when her elder daughter entered the room. Hurriedly, she thrust the material into her work-basket, but Sir Mark had already launched into his single-handed despatch of the dreaded Black Gentleman. Leonora was privately of the opinion that he would have cut a much better figure if he had not waited until the highwayman was presenting a back view, but at this point, Lady Constance went into mild hysterics.

Entirely forgetting the exquisite sensibility she had previously displayed, Leonora stamped her foot and informed him tartly that her mama would now be imagining a host of predators ready to swoop on her every time she ventured beyond the doorstep. Briskly directing her sister to fetch the smelling salts, she straightened Lady Constance's turban, and slapped her hands with what Sir Mark considered uneasily to be unnecessary vigour.

Maria returned with the smelling salts, and these Leonora applied ruthlessly to Lady Constance's nostrils, causing the poor lady's eyes to water profusely, and bringing forth a protesting moan. Recovering fully, she clasped her lamb to her ample bosom.

'My love! What did he say? What did he do?'

'He apologised for having alarmed us.'

'Nothing more?'

'No,' Leonora said, conveniently forgetting the rest of the episode. 'I told him he was welcome to anything he could find!'

Lady Constance shuddered, and felt again for her salts. Sir Mark's notions of a suitable bride would not encompass a female who would descend to bandying words with a highwayman: Leonora was dispelling his illusions with every breath she uttered. How to find another suitor in this district for a daughter who had not even been presented she was at her wits' end to know. She wondered despairingly if she could give Leonora a nip without being observed, but even this was denied her. She closed her eyes again, and lay back on the cushions, Leonora mechanically righting the inevitable slide of the turban.

Mr. Revell, who had listened without much interest to Sir Mark's narrative, viewed his wife's vapours with an experienced eye, and helped himself to a liberal pinch of snuff.

'No need to make a pother,' he said, interrupting Sir Mark's apologies. He dusted off his lapels and regarded Lady Constance tolerantly. 'You grow accustomed to it in twenty-four years.' He patted his wife's shoulder. 'Come into the other room and join Simon. They'll do better without us here.' He led the way out, and as the door shut behind them, Lady Constance sat up with a snap.

'I thought you were putting it on,' Leonora observed with satisfaction.

'Putting it on! I was never so in earnest in my life! Leonora, how *could* you. To actually stamp your foot when I swear he was on the very brink of offering for you. Such good fortune can never come our way again. Even the vicar's married.'

'I wouldn't,' Leonora said, with deadly emphasis, 'marry your precious Sir Mark if he was the last man left alive!'

Lady Constance said faintly, 'But all that money! And Maria could be brought out.' She struggled to a more upright position to lend force to her statement. 'Leonora, you *must!*'

Leonora felt Maria's reproachful brown eyes on her, and turned round to glare. 'No,' she snapped. 'He's odious and pompous, and seven and thirty if he's a day, and I will not spend the rest of my life simpering and watching my tongue just to suit his notions of propriety!'

Lady Constance gave another moan, and sank down again. 'What shall we do?'

'Sell something?' Leonora suggested flippantly.

'You know perfectly well we can't. I wonder we're left with enough furniture to sit on!' Lady Constance, who was the daughter of an earl, dwelt for a moment on the wealthy baronet she had turned down in favour of Mr. Revell, and on the plight of her elder daughter, who should, by rights, have enjoyed her first London season.

'Oh, go to bed, Leonora, you'll change your mind in the morning, I know you will.'

'That creature sat there on his horse as though he'd been stuffed, when I might have been in the direst peril, which just shows the true extent of his regard for me.'

'He wouldn't have served any useful purpose by getting himself shot,' Lady Constance pointed out with simple reason.

'If he really cared for me, he wouldn't have considered it!'

'Well who else is likely to offer for you, situated as we are?'

'I'd rather die a spinster!' This was uttered with complete finality, and leaving her afflicted parent seething, Leonora stalked up to her room.

Mr. Revell entered through the still open door, and his wife struggled to her feet.

'Maria, my love, I must have a few private words with your father.' She waited until Maria had reluctantly removed herself, then said, 'Edmund, where is Sir Mark?'

'In the library,' he replied indifferently. 'Why?'

'Something dreadful has happened! Leonora declares she won't marry him!'

'Does she?' Mr. Revell said, with more interest. 'Never did care for the fellow.' He lowered himself into a chair. 'Can't understand why you were so keen to push it. Don't like the stock. I knew his father,' he added in explanation. 'What made her change her mind?'

'I don't know,' Lady Constance wailed. 'Some nonsense about him sitting his horse as though he were stuffed when she was in direst peril.'

Mr. Revell shook his head in bewilderment and stretched out his legs. 'At least,' he said, with pleasureable anticipation, 'I can stop being so damned polite to Finchley.'

'That isn't the point, Edmund.' Lady Constance was almost in tears. 'Apart from being so tall, Leonora is twenty years of age, and living so remote, with hardly a card party within fifteen miles, how is she likely to meet another eligible man?'

Mr. Revell brought his bushy brows together, and regarded her for a moment. 'Too early to tell you anything at present,' he said abruptly, 'but it may be that our fortunes are on the mend. All I can say, my dear, is no need to despair yet.' He took another pinch of snuff, liberally decorating his waistcoat in the process, and, heedless of Lady Constance's frustrated gaze, dosed off to sleep.

2

Mr. Paul Rochford read the letter through twice and swore.

'Brookes, I want a note taken round to Mr. Barnethorpe's lodgings. No, dammit, I'll go myself.'

'Anything else, sir?' Brookes deftly caught a hairbrush as it slid off the dressing table, and regarded his employer tolerantly.

Heavily preoccupied, Mr. Rochford did not hear him. There was a faint stirring of uneasiness in the region of his stomach. He finished dressing and glanced at the clock. Mr. Barnethorpe was a notoriously late riser, but he judged that by now he had given him enough time to be up.

He found him blearily regarding himself in the mirror.

'Thought you might not be intelligent yet,' Mr. Rochford said, peering at the reflected image. 'Never mind. I came to say this afternoon's off. Sorry, but something urgent's turned up, and I have to go out of town.'

Mr. Barnethorpe, after inspecting his tongue, parted the lids and examined an eyeball with detached interest. 'When will you be back?'

'As soon as I can. Sorry to let you down.'

'As a matter of fact, I'm not feeling quite my best,' Mr. Barnethorpe confessed. 'Bad news?'

'That,' Mr. Rochford replied, quelling a sense of fore-boding, 'remains to be seen.'

He returned to his house and gave orders for his horses to be brought round in half an hour, and wisely refraining from giving any explanations, drove out of town.

Before he reached his destination a fine sleet had begun to fall, and by the time he reached the Bird-in-Hand the light was failing rapidly and he was numb with cold. He thankfully handed over the curricle to an ostler, and gave instructions for the care of the tired chestnuts before entering the taproom.

Inside, he stood by the fireplace, irresolute. The room was warm and cheerful, and the landlord, industriously polishing glasses by the bar, struck him as an eminently respectable fellow, a positive champion of the law. Mr. Rochford was not happy with any form of intrigue, and his feeling of uneasiness deepened. He stood for so long that in the end the landlord came over to him, and after a measuring look asked if he would be the gentleman come to see Mr. Wallace.

Relieved, Mr. Rochford confessed that he was, and was conducted to an upstairs parlour. As the door closed behind the landlord, he said, with strong feeling, 'I've put poor old Barney off, and driven all the way from London without a change of cattle on a damned cold day for you.'

Captain Matheson grinned. 'Afraid of someone picking up your trail at the posthouses?' He pulled up a chair and leaned his good arm on the table. 'Paul, I want you to do something for me.'

'I'll not stop a coach,' Mr. Rochford said suspiciously. 'And who gave you that shoulder?'

'Mark Finchley.'

Mr. Rochford let out a strangled exclamation. 'Well, it must be the first time in his life he's ever hit anything! What do you want me to do?'

'Weren't you going to France some time soon?'

'Taking some things over for my father,' Mr. Rochford said warily. 'Why?'

'I,' said the captain, spacing his words for effect, 'am about to re-enter society!'

Mr. Rochford rose rapidly to his feet.

'No, no,' the captain soothed. 'There will be nothing desperate. Let me explain my simple little plan of campaign.'

'I've been following your simple little plans of campaign ever since I was at Eton, and they usually ended up with someone thrashing the backside off me,' Mr. Rochford said bitterly.

Feeling that a measure of brandy might dispel this unnecessarily pessimistic viewpoint, the captain rang for Joe. Mr. Rochford watched with starting eyes as he joined them at the table.

'He's in the plot,' the captain explained. 'Now for the time-table. I shall go to France ahead of you, and establish myself in, say, Le Havre. We'll arrange an accidental meeting—we can work out the details nearer the date—and all you have to do is recognise me in a public spot and filter the news back to England.'

'Why do I have to recognise you?' Mr. Rochford said, bewildered. 'Known you best part of my life!'

'Because I don't remember you! I've lost my memory, due to my severe head wound.'

'It's affected your reason as well,' Mr. Rochford said indignantly. 'Who'll believe a damned silly story like that?'

'Everybody, by the time we've finished,' the captain

said, accepting these strictures patiently. 'It's perfectly true that I suffered a temporary loss of memory, and it's not unheard of for it to continue. Look at Meredith!'

'That's true,' Mr. Rochford admitted. 'Funny business. Didn't recognise his own wife for six months. Mind you,' he added fair-mindedly. 'I'd be tempted to do the same thing myself. Long-nosed female with rabbit teeth. He married her because he was up to his ears in debt, and she'd been on the market so long, no one else would have her. Must have been pretty desperate though.'

The captain grinned, then pondered for a moment. 'Perhaps it would be better if we came back together.'

'It might be better for you, but I ain't ending up on Tyburn with you,' Mr. Rochford said frankly. 'And what about the Black Gentleman? No one hears of him again, and you suddenly turn up. They ain't all fools on the town, and somebody might add two and two.'

'If I know Mark Finchley, it will be all over the clubs by now that he's hit me. The Black Gentleman is either dead or disabled.'

'I don't like it,' Mr. Rochford said, shaking his head. 'And what will you do with Caesar? Unless you're intending to ride him in Hyde Park,' he added bitterly.

'I'll see to him,' Joe put in. 'A farmer friend of mine further south will take him. He rides about seventeen stone, and he has a job getting anything reasonable that's up to his weight. It'll be well out of the area.'

'No one could swear to him anyway,' the captain said. 'Bay gelding, all black points. He's not distinctive.'

Mr. Rochford looked helpless. 'It seems risky to me. Why is Joe fool enough to come into it?'

'He was my batman.' The captain was amused. 'Did

you think you were taking part in a complete fairy-tale? Someone tried to beat my brains in while I was gathering information for Intelligence. When the regiment was disbanded after Waterloo, Joe sold the horses and set out to find me. Everyone else thought I must be dead.'

'And a good job I knew where you was heading for,' Joe grunted. 'What with me not speaking the language much, and him going about all secret, if he hadn't been uncommon tall, I'd never have found him. And I didn't know he was going to start up this caper when I fetched him home.'

'Never knew you were in Intelligence,' Mr. Rochford muttered, mortified.

'I wasn't encouraged to tell people,' the captain · explained apologetically, 'but due to my mama being French, I have such a beautiful accent that they gave me one or two little jobs. Now the point is this. As far as the regiment was concerned, I was missing, and I travelled on false papers all the time, so there isn't anyone, anywhere, who could identify me. Even the family who took me in didn't know who I was, and since they were Royalists in a strong Bonapartist district, they didn't give it out that they were harbouring me.'

'If they'd known you for as long as I have, they wouldn't have harboured you at all,' Mr. Rochford commented. 'That's all very well, but I knew you were back in England the day you stopped my coach and demanded my valuables. I haven't actually heard of anyone else recognising you, but I keep telling you they ain't all half-witted.'

'I knew it was you when I stopped you,' the captain said, laughing heartily. 'I saw your chestnuts. Besides, the place is thick with Black Gentlemen. I've been credited with every hold-up south of London. God help anyone who tried to investigate them all.'

'I don't know,' Mr. Rochford said doubtfully. 'There's something about the way you sit your horse, and they haven't all got your height.'

But every objection he raised was overruled, and the unhappy Mr. Rochford found himself carried along with a plan which he felt was fraught with the possibilities of mischance.

Of a naturally cautious disposition, the carefully rehearsed meeting in the main thoroughfare of Le Havre tried his nerves to the full, and just when he thought his ordeal was at an end Captain Matheson announced his intention of continuing on to Paris.

'Paris!' Mr. Rochford's head shot up with an expression of pure horror. 'But it will be full of English!'

'Just what we need!'

Bitterly, Mr. Rochford gave him to understand that it had always been his ambition to die in his own bed, and they set out the next day for what proved to be the most harrowing eight days of his existence. The English Army of Occupation in Paris included several officers with whom the captain was personally acquainted, and Mr. Rochford retired to his bed each night in a sweat of terror, reliving every awkward moment and wondering with despair what the morrow held to torment him.

However, at the end of eight days the captain was satisfied and they made their way back to the coast. Mr. Rochford fell into the boat almost gibbering with relief.

'Never spent such a wearing fortnight in my life!' He shuddered at the recollection. 'Paris! My God, I thought we were undone there!'

'I know you did,' the captain said, wholly unperturbed. 'But we are obviously destined to be successful. Assisted, of course, by my careful arrangements.'

Still following his plans, he quietly re-established himself in London. He visited his former tailor, who dropped the news to successive clients, presented himself at his bankers and lawyers, and put in an appearance at his old clubs. As he had forecast to Mr. Rochford, the report of his reappearance had preceded him from the continent, and the astonishment at his return was considerably lessened.

He answered all questions with the fluency of a man who has nothing to hide, assuring everyone that he was now fully recovered; he could recall almost everything, except, of course the period following his injury, which, he pointed out to Mr. Rochford in private, was reasonably true.

Within a very short space of time, people were saying that they had always known he couldn't be dead, and in White's one man clapped him on the shoulder and said he wouldn't believe old Louis had been killed off unless he had attended his funeral. His commanding officers in the recent war were glad to know he had survived, but had no further interest in him from an official standpoint, since his regiment was no more.

Louis Matheson, now a private citizen, was well pleased, and congratulated himself on his delicate handling of the whole affair.

There was then an occurrence which, he was forced to admit, his planning had played no part in. Just as he was well established on the social scene, his cousin Robert James Matheson, sixth Earl of Everard, chose to leave it.

He was discovered dead in his bed in a room full of smoke, but without so much as a singe upon his person.

The footman who conducted the doctor to the room where he had been laid marvelled over it with dour satisfaction.

'Not a mark on him! Just like the devil had snatched him up!'

'Well he didn't,' the doctor snapped. He had been called from his bed at an unseasonable hour to attend his least popular patient, and, in addition, had received a measure of water from one of the fire buckets. 'He was asphyxiated by the smoke. What I can't understand is why he wasn't roused by it!'

The footman coughed. 'Myself and the valet put him to bed. I doubt anything would have woken him before morning.'

'Drunk again, was he?' He dropped the sheet back over the late earl. 'Well, there's nothing more I can do for him in any event. What caused the fire?'

'As far as we was able to ascertain, the chimney caught afire, and there was a bad fall of burning soot.' The footman's eyes narrowed with relish. 'He didn't come nigh the place best part of the year. Left it to go to rack and ruin. I can't remember when them chimneys was last swept.'

'Poetic,' the doctor commented, collecting his things back into the bag. 'I'll see Lady Everard before I leave. I presume she is already aware of what has occurred?'

The footman schooled his face to a careful blank. 'Someone has been sent to the Dower House to inform her ladyship.'

The doctor raised his eyebrows.

'Her ladyship always took up residence in the Dower House during his lordship's visits.'

'Then it's fortunate his visits were infrequent.' The doctor looked round the room. 'His cousin inherits all this, I collect. I remember him as a lad. He might bring about some improvements.'

Calling for his gig, he shrugged himself into his greatcoat and disappeared into the night, to offer advice, since comfort was not called for, to the widow.

The gist of all this was relayed to Louis Matheson, first by his lawyers, and then, in more detail, by Mr. Rochford.

'Well, well,' the new peer murmured, 'I can think of one or two little embarrassments if this had occurred before we put our plans into action. People would be bound to remark that my reappearance hard on the heels of his death was a trifle fortuitous.'

He began to laugh, and Mr. Rochford regarded him doubtfully.

'Just a thought. As Earl of Everard, I shall be welcomed everywhere with open arms, and last month I held up three members of White's!'

Mr. Rochford clutched his head.

Accompanied still by his faithful ally, who nobly declared that his time was his own, and London was flat at this season, the new earl took up residence at Abbotsford Hall.

Mr. Rochford's motives were not, in fact, as pure as he made out. He had no desire to be left behind to face questions he doubted his ability to extricate himself from, and there was also the possibility that if his mother heard he was still in town she might command his presence at the ancestral home. Neither prospect appealed, but as he stood in the dank, December air, and surveyed the depressing aspect of Abbotsford, he felt he could have striven harder to find some other alternative.

'Ain't there a decent inn we could put up at?' he suggested hopefully.

'You'll stay and suffer with me. Come on, we'd better see if the stables are fit for the postboys to put the horses in.'

An undergroom conducted them round the dusty, ill-kept stalls and loose boxes. They were largely deserted, the only horses in evidence being two hacks, apparently used by the dowager countess and her daughter, two hacks belonging to the late earl, and the coach horses. The earl took a handful of hay from a rack and wrinkled his nose at the smell of must, and Mr. Rochford, staring round him in disgust, said, 'I was going to send for my cattle, but I ain't having them housed in this!' He prodded one of the divisions in the stalls, and it broke apart, rotten with damp. 'No wish to be rude about your relatives, dear boy, but our pigs are better kept at home.'

It occurred to him for the first time that the neglect might be due to a lack of money, and he ventured a diffident enquiry.

'No. It was merely that he disliked spending it,' the earl said cheerfully. 'I've been through all that with the lawyers.' He closed the stable doors behind them. 'Let's go and see what the house has in store for us.'

'Has it always been like this?' Mr. Rochford said, his disapproval deepening with every dilapidated outbuilding.

'I don't know. I haven't been here since I was eight.'

'If I was heir to it, I'd have popped over to look at it every now and then.'

'I've never thought about it much,' the earl said, after consideration. 'Caroline's not much above my age. She could always have come up with a son. Or my cousin could have poisoned her and married again!'

'She's been causing a to-do with Matthew Digby for years. Barney says she was holding hands with him in the Dower House before Robert had been dead a week.'

The earl murmured something noncommittal. He had been startled to discover from the lawyers that he had been appointed guardian to Caroline's seventeen-year-old daughter. Her dowry was meagre, and if the dowager countess caused any open scandals it would obviously prejudice her daughter's chances of marriage. The late earl and his wife had lived in a state of mutual antipathy for the eighteen years of their marriage, and the will had been his last act of retaliation. Lord Everard wished that he had thought up some other revenge. Caroline, as he remembered her, was a formidable woman.

They had now reached the top of the steps leading to the front door, and through the tall Palladian columns were afforded a panoramic view of the waterlogged countryside.

'Know anything about drainage, Paul?' the earl enquired, his cheerfulness unimpaired.

Mr. Rochford confessed to ignorance, but volunteered the opinion that if the house had been built lower down they'd have got their feet wet by now.

'I shall have to pick a few brains. I wonder how one gets hold of the steward?'

Whatever knowledge the earl lacked concerning the running of an estate, he more than made up for by his organisation. Within a remarkably short space of time he gathered about him a competent staff and began repairs, and he and Mr. Rochford rode round the land and farms, ordering the digging of ditches, new gates and fences, and much needed repairs to roofs and barns.

His activities brought a flood of work to the local people. The village carpenter, in his undreamed-of prosperity, was able to marry off his second daughter in a manner that was the envy of his friends, and the village blacksmith was forced to hire a young man to assist him with the huge wrought-iron gates that were to grace the drive to Abbotsford.

Inside the house, the volubly objecting Mr. Rochford was harried from room to room by an army of workmen, and protested that there was nowhere he could sit down.

'Damned if I see why you can't get one room straight before you start on the next,' he complained. 'I put a book down yesterday and I haven't seen it since.'

The earl, who was watching a workman delicately gilding a frieze, said sympathetically that he was sorry to find him reduced to reading.

'Too tired to do anything else after you've dragged me over muddy fields all day long,' Mr. Rochford said simply.

The earl, reviewing his achievements with pardonable pride, was satisfied that everything could now be left under the control of his steward. Only in the matter of the countess had he been forced to admit defeat.

By shameless bribery he had induced her to remain at

the Dower House with the pretty, pale-skinned Sarah, and even to take a cousin to live with her for propriety's sake. His error was in using the Dower House stables and coach-house while the main stables were being repaired. A few days later carriage and pair, together with the countess and her daughter, were gone, leaving the hysterical cousin to face the earl.

'Devil fly away with the woman!' he fumed to Mr. Rochford. 'There'll be a rare scandal over this!'

'Fetch her back,' Mr. Rochford suggested helpfully.

'I should be grateful if you could tell me where to look!'

Displaying rare acumen, Mr. Rochford said, 'Find Digby, and she won't be far away.'

'She wouldn't come. And I can hardly drag Sarah, screaming, from her mother's arms!'

'If there's nothing you can do about it, myself, I'd say it was more important that you engage a new cook.'

The earl agreed that it was of paramount importance, and promptly descended to the kitchens, Mr. Rochford, still protesting, behind him.

'You ain't got any dignity, that's your trouble. Why can't you send for the fellow to come upstairs, like any normal human being would?'

'Because you have reminded me that I have never seen the kitchens,' the earl returned. 'And I'll lay you any money it's a female.'

So it turned out to be. Scurrying amongst her ancient equipment, they found the poor little soul who had been pressed into service on the abrupt departure of the chef, and who greeted the prospect of returning to her normal duties with undisguised relief.

Feeling that a prudent man would depart while kitchen alterations were in progress, the earl suggested to Mr. Rochford that they should open up the London house.

'Nothing much doing at this time of year,' Mr. Rochford said diffidently.

'I was thinking more along the lines of furnishing and decorating than social engagements,' the earl admitted.

'I ain't coming to stay with you in another muddle like this one,' Mr. Rochford said indignantly. 'Rather go and stay with my parents. Come to think, I might as well, and get it over with.'

'Such unfilial reluctance!'

Mr. Rochford, an only son of twenty-nine, took on a hunted look. 'You don't know what it's like. My mother's mad keen to marry me off. Last time I went some silly female misunderstood something I said and practically had me to the altar!' He looked hopefully at the earl. 'You could come with me. Help draw their fire.'

Considering the real nobility with which he had endured the conditions at Abbotsford, the earl felt it was the least he could do, and in the event it worked better than either of them had foreseen. As heir to his father's wealth, Mr. Rochford had long been the target for ambitious mamas, but to his amusement the earl found that his title held an additional lure.

Mrs. Rochford, after carefully gathering about her a selection of the season's most eligible damsels, was forced to sit by and watch them cluster round the earl, trilling songs to him while he turned over their music, and languishing glances at him over the dinner table. She ground her teeth in chagrin as her son went his way, free and unfettered, and the earl conducted his genteel flirtations under her roof.

One girl she had earmarked as especially suitable, and into Miss Catherine Harford's ear particularly did Lord Everard murmur dulcet compliments, and gratify with leisured walks in the shrubbery. Mrs. Rochford, reasonably astute, was not much consoled by the reflection that the complacent smile would be wiped from the Hon. Mrs. Harford's face if she knew that the earl's attentions were nothing more than a plot between himself and her son.

Meanwhile, the earl was well entertained. The lovely Catherine was more amusing than most of her decorous contemporaries, and her thick-fringed eyes occasionally held a calculating gleam which successfully banished any twinge of conscience. But her beauty was undeniable, and the earl, musing on his new found attraction for the fair sex, parted from her with tantalising half-promises. Winding her copper ringlets through his fingers, he smiled down at her, and Catherine, deeming it her moment of triumph, raised her face for his kiss. The earl, however, had no intention of committing himself, and brushing her hand with his lips in a formal gesture of farewell, strolled away to take leave of his hostess.

Catherine stared after him, baffled and frustrated, no longer sure whether it was his handsome face and charm that drew her or the cold-blooded consideration of his wealth and title.

She moved to the window to watch, as he and Mr. Rochford walked across the drive to meet the curricle. While the groom hung on to the chestnuts, they held a brief argument as to who should drive, and she saw the earl's quick smile flash as he climbed up and took the reins, forcing Mr. Rochford to ride passenger behind his own horses.

Tears started suddenly to her eyes. Accustomed to taking her pick of her admirers, it was a new experience to find herself in the reverse position, and she determined that he should take her seriously.

It was nearly six weeks, however, before they met again. She had developed the habit of quickly glancing round every gathering as she entered and of accepting invitations where he might be present. Then, on an ordinary shopping expedition, she found herself face to face with him.

He invited her to drive in the park, and biting her lip in frustration, she was forced to refuse. Due to his absence from the London scene, the Hon. Mrs. Harford had abandoned the hopes she cherished, and encouraged her daughter instead, to lend an ear to the protestations of Sir Mark Finchley, who, though immensely wealthy, could not stand comparison with the earl.

Lord Everard did not appear to be roused to a fever of jealousy by her disclosure that she was riding with Sir Mark, but they were hardly inside the gates of the park before he came up beside them, mounted on a long-tailed black.

He towered over Sir Mark, who, aware that he appeared to disadvantage, also noted that his companion had undergone a remarkable change. Catherine was flushed, and had suddenly acquired a vivacious sparkle. He bent a lowering look upon the earl.

'I didn't know you were back in town.'

'Alas, I didn't know Miss Harford was back in town,'

the earl returned gaily. Sir Mark's attitude reminded him strongly of a dog with a bone, and, alight with devilment, he lingered beside them. As Sir Mark grew more curt, so his gallantry increased, and Catherine sparkled more brightly.

Eventually, to Sir Mark's relief, he was hailed by a friend, and with a flourish of his hat and a bow to Catherine he cantered away.

Sir Mark watched him with a frown. His process of thought was not quick, but there was something about the earl's smooth seat, and the negligent way he picked a path one-handed through the equestrian press, that stirred a faint recollection. He saw himself pursuing the highwayman through the patchy moonlight, picturing the way he swayed with his horse round the curves of the bridle path.

He said abruptly. 'When did that fellow reappear in town?'

Catherine's mouth dropped slightly. However capricious she chose to be with her escorts, she had never, until this moment, been interrupted in the middle of a sentence.

'If you are referring to Lord Everard I first met him when Mama and I attended Mrs. Rochford's Christmas gathering.'

'He was seen about just before his cousin died,' Sir Mark said, still pondering to himself. 'Everybody thought he'd been killed until then.'

'If we are to discuss his past history, I should perhaps inform you that I am already acquainted with it,' Catherine said waspishly.

Sir Mark regarded her blankly while the realisation dawned on him that the whole idea was too preposterous for utterance. Nevertheless, it remained in his mind.

In the succeeding days it seemed that he could never escort Catherine and her mother to a ball or to the play without the earl appearing somewhere on the scene to mar his enjoyment.

There was no doubt that Catherine looked upon him with favour, and in the face of this threat Sir Mark hastened to secure her by obtaining her mother's consent to their marriage.

But the Hon. Mrs. Harford, showing her teeth in a smile, had no intention of committing her daughter while there was a possibility of Lord Everard being brought up to the mark.

Catherine was only in her first season; she must be allowed to see a little more of the world. Punctuating her remarks with displays of teeth, she assured Sir Mark that she would be happy to see her daughter wedded to him, but he would understand—her only child—herself a widow . . . She dabbed the corners of her eyes with a handkerchief.

Sir Mark boiled helplessly. With great skill, Mrs. Harford had neither accepted nor rebuffed him, and he was perfectly aware of her motives.

It was no great comfort to him Lord Everard was dividing his favours. While his flirtation with Catherine provided food for the gossip-mongers, he appeared to derive considerable enjoyment from the company of several other young ladies, including some of the dashing matrons nearer his own age. Neither was it a comfort to find him equally popular in exclusively male circles.

Sir Mark was a great lover of sport, and every year got up his own shooting parties on one of his extensive estates, but it was seldom he managed to bring down a bird. He hunted with the foremost packs, but in spite of his expensive thoroughbreds, was always left behind. Conscious of a developing paunch, he painstakingly attended Gentleman Jackson's famous boxing saloon, but was woefully short-winded and slow on his feet.

Admittedly he had a large circle of friends amongst the less discriminating and those who did not aspire to remarkable feats in the sporting field, and formerly he had been perfectly content with these. He found it galled him, however, to see the earl accepted into the highest strata of society, and moving with equal ease in the sporting circles and the ballroom.

Lord Everard was acknowledged to be a brilliant rider and whip. His accuracy at Manton's Shooting Gallery was already famed, and with his powerful frame and tremendous reach he was a formidable boxer.

If he had not made Catherine Harford the object of his gallantries, Sir Mark would not have grudged him these attributes; until now he had been largely indifferent to the achievements of others, and his own lack of prowess in sporting company had never disturbed him. He might even have ignored the suspicion that this darling of society was none other than the notorious Black Gentleman, but goaded by jealousy, his animosity simmered slowly to the boil.

On one occasion they happened to attend Jackson's saloon at the same time, and he was able to see the earl in action. For a large man he was remarkably light on his feet, and though matched against an opponent of comparable size and weight, emerged from the bout unmarked and only slightly breathless.

'Good science,' the man next to Sir Mark commented.

Sir Mark nodded, without replying. During the bout his attention had been caught by a recent scar just below the earl's left shoulder. Ignoring the other man, he moved forward and placed himself squarely in front of the earl, staring hard at the area of puckered skin. His very attitude amounted to rudeness, and several of the company began to look surprised.

'I was wondering,' he said finally, 'how you got your scar!'

Lord Everard raised his brows. 'Merely one of Bonaparte's adherents expressing an opinion.'

'It looks more recent to me,' Sir Mark said deliberately.

Their eyes met, and comprehension gleamed in the earl's. Mr. Rochford, who had been on the point of joining them, stood rooted to the spot, and the earl's sparring partner glanced enquiringly from one to the other.

'Does it?' the earl said gently. 'Perhaps that is because it broke open again before it was properly healed. It was remarkably troublesome for such a minor injury.'

'It looks like a bullet wound to me!'

'But my dear fellow, it was a bullet wound.' The earl was amused. 'Whoever said it wasn't?'

Sir Mark flushed, and turned on his heel. One or two people stared after him, and the Hon. Frederick Brereton lounged up, draping a towel round his shoulders.

'What on earth was all that about, Louis?'

The earl grinned, and Mr. Rochford unfroze and entered the group.

'I don't think Mark Finchley likes me!'

'I don't blame him,' Freddy Brereton said frankly. 'If you don't stop treading on his toes with the Harford girl, he'll probably put a bullet through you himself!'

There was a general shout of derision, and one man recalled that he had been with him once when he brought a partridge down. 'Never seen a fellow so surprised in my life. Mind you, he claims he shot that highwayman—the Black Gentleman or whatever they call him, and it's a fact that he ain't been seen since. Could have been a lucky shot, I suppose.'

Mr. Rochford went rigid once more, and swallowed hard. His brain had assimilated the fact that if Sir Mark could identify the earl as the highwayman he shot, their main defence was gone.

'Marchant says he was held up by him just after Christmas,' he said desperately.

'Ah, probably Finchley just winged him then,' Freddy remarked.

'And probably it's all moonshine,' someone else said impatiently. 'Isn't anybody coming to the club?'

Sir Mark, seething, had flung out of the saloon. He started towards White's, then checked as he realised that the earl and his companions would probably go there. Damning under his breath, he made for a less exclusive haunt, and fell in with one of his intimates in the entrance hall.

Mr. Fullard was prepared to put up with anything for the sake of Sir Mark's patronage and the prospect of living several weeks of the year under his roof. He regarded him sympathetically, and asked what had occurred to put him out of temper.

'That damned fellow Everard!'

Well aware of the situation, Mr. Fullard preserved a discreet silence while Sir Mark called for a bottle and brooded over his wrongs. His well-meant suggestion of a game of cards was badly received, and he sat in silence as Sir Mark, normally a moderate drinker, worked his way steadily down the bottle, drinking two glasses to one of his own. His slightly pompous manner completely gone, Sir Mark tilted the empty bottle and called for another.

Unable to think of a safe topic of conversation for a man seemingly intent of getting castaway halfway through the afternoon, Mr. Fullard cleared his throat unhappily.

Sir Mark glared at him. 'He might be the Earl of Everard now, but I've known him any number of years when he was plain Louis Matheson! Gives himself airs!'

Anxious to please, Mr. Fullard nodded agreement.

'I could tell them all something about him . . . suspected it for weeks . . . saw the proof today. You're the same. Don't believe it!'

'Don't know what it is I'm not supposed to believe,' Mr. Fullard ventured carefully.

'Wouldn't believe it if I told you. Recognised him as soon as I saw him in the park. Seen where I put the bullet in his arm!'

'You put a bullet through Everard!' Mr. Fullard said, aghast.

Sir Mark leaned forward and prodded him. 'Surprises you, doesn't it? I put a bullet through him because it was night, and he was all dressed up in black with a mask over his face! He's the Black Gentleman, that's who your precious Lord Everard is!' Mr. Fullard's jaw dropped, and Sir Mark waved his hand irritably. 'You're the same. Won't believe it!'

Mr. Fullard, who had never aspired to the earl's set, and knew which side his bread was buttered, vigorously disclaimed disbelief, and Sir Mark, his gaze becoming a trifle unfocussed, reached for the bottle again. His hand slid past it, and Mr. Fullard, his mind in a state of shock, absently guided it towards its objective.

'Tell you something else. He knows that I know!'

Mr. Fullard made inarticulate noises. Anxious to know more, he was, at the same time, unwilling to be the recipient of confidences Sir Mark was undoubtedly going to regret when he was sober.

'I tell you, he knows that I know,' Sir Mark repeated. He toppled slowly over the table, and Mr. Fullard, released from his trance, glanced round and discovered an interested group behind him, their ears on the stretch.

'I'll call him a hackney,' he said hurriedly.

Between them he and the doorman assisted Sir Mark into the vehicle, and he gave the jarvey the direction. He walked slowly back into the clubroom. The conversation ceased as he went in; one or two people made as if to speak to him. Mr. Fullard, in whom discretion had always been the better part of valour, hastily reversed and made for the street. Behind him he heard the buzz of conversation break out again.

3

The unfortunate repercussions of Leonora's behaviour
were felt almost at once. There was a noticeable waning of
enthusiasm on Sir Mark's part when next he called upon
them. Indeed, Lady Constance doubted whether he would
have called at all if it had not been a firm engagement
fixed earlier in the week.

'Well that settles it once and for all,' Leonora said with
satisfaction, when he had gone.

Lady Constance, inclined to be tearful, groped for her
handkerchief. 'It is all very well for you to take that attitude, Leonora, but you haven't considered the benefit it
might have been to the rest of us.'

Leonora looked puzzled, and Mr. Revell lowered his
journal. 'I collect your mother is talking about settlements.'

'Settlements!' Leonora gasped indignantly. 'Do you
mean you would have sold me like a . . . a horse!'

'Nothing of the sort,' Lady Constance said, flushing. 'It
is not such an unusual arrangement, after all. I could
name you quite a few families who have not thought it beneath them to come to some agreement.'

'You may call it by whatever name you choose,' Leo-

43

nora retorted. 'I should still object to being bought like so much livestock!'

'The gentlemen don't object to taking the dowry,' Lady Constance pointed out. 'It wouldn't be so very different after all.'

'Well I doubt whether he would have been prepared to pay,' Leonora said dispassionately. 'He doesn't appear to have been wildly enamoured of me after all.'

'The question doesn't arise,' Mr. Revell said. 'For one thing, matters didn't reach such a point, and for another, even if the suggestion had been made, I should not have permitted it.'

With oppressed mien, Lady Constance reached for her handkerchief again. 'But it might have solved all our problems!'

'Leonora would not agree with you, and, besides, I don't care to have my problems solved by such a means. I've told you before, Constance, that things may not be as bad as they appear. I'm waiting for confirmation of certain things before I divulge them, but if this venture of mine turns out as I hope, we shall be in very much more comfortable circumstances.'

Lady Constance stared at him, hideous visions arising of them all being involved in some precarious gamble. When they were first married, Mr. Revell had been heir to a reasonable estate, and considered a suitable, though not brilliant, match for the daughter of Lord Trenchard. It was unfortunate that his father, at an age when he should have been toasting his feet at a fire, had conceived a totally unpredictable passion for all forms of play. Happily, he had succumbed to a chill before he could dispose of the entire estate, but Mr. Revell's depleted inheritance was the root of all their monetary troubles.

'Edmund!' she said, with urgent dismay. 'Edmund, you haven't been *gambling*!'

'Gambling! Of course I haven't,' he said. 'Whatever gave you that idea. No, this is a business venture.' He returned to his paper, and Leonora tweaked it out of his grasp impatiently.

'Papa, don't be so exasperating! What sort of business venture?'

Mr. Revell sighed. 'Daughter, it is by no means positive yet, and I am not going to tell you more until I am certain of my facts. You would none of you thank me for raising false hopes, so you may give me back my paper.'

'Do you think,' Leonora breathed, hardly daring to put it into words, 'do you think there will be sufficient for us to go to London?'

She and Lady Constance waited, with bated breath, as he looked at them with amusement. 'Certainly, but whether it will be in the style your mother would wish is another matter.' He broke off as Leonora smothered the top of his head with kisses, and danced wildly round the room with Lady Constance until she squeaked protestingly that she was breathless.

Deposited, panting, on the sofa, she said, 'It is really true, Edmund? I shall be able to take the girls to London?'

'Yes—though I've told you I don't know how much there will be to spare. I shouldn't have mentioned it to you at all until I had the complete figures to hand, but that may be a week and more, and quite frankly, my dear, with the dismal state you're in over Leonora, I don't think I could bear another week of it!'

Leonora kissed him again. 'I don't care if we lodge in a garret, just so long as we go.'

'Yes, but one would be bound to meet the wrong sort of people there,' Lady Constance pointed out practically. She looked hopefully at her spouse. 'If we could perhaps hire a house?'

But Mr. Revell refused to be drawn further, and they had to contain themselves in patience for almost a fort-night, at which time he gathered his family together to an-nounce the welcome change in their financial situation.

Aware that he had not been entirely open before about the precise nature of his business venture, he had foreseen the possibility of his lady's reaction. While his children re-garded him with various degrees of gratification, Lady Constance heard him out in stunned silence.

'Trade!' Her voice rose to a shriek. 'Edmund, have you been engaging in *trade*?'

'Of course I have,' he said with some irritation. The past eighteen months had been something of a strain. To finance his scheme, he had been forced to mortgage every inch of land he possessed, and his nights had been trou-bled by thoughts of their future if he failed in this under-taking which was so foreign to his upbringing and breed-ing.

'If it should ever leak out we shall be ruined!' Lady Constance said tragically. 'Do you want to see your daughters married to some city merchant?'

Mr. Revell considered, reminding her that she had re-cently bewailed the fact that they were not likely to receive any offers at all, but contented himself with pointing out that no one need know where their money came from. 'Simon and I have never mentioned it. You and the girls won't.'

Lady Constance turned to glare at her son. 'Simon already knew?'

'I knew from the start,' Simon said cheerfully.

'I had to mortgage the land, so it was only fair to bring the boy into it.'

Lady Constance's bosom swelled with gathering wrath. 'You told Simon, and didn't discuss it with *me!*'

Mr. Revell said hastily, 'Women don't understand these things.'

'I had no idea you understood them yourself,' Lady Constance returned, with unusual acidity.

'It makes no matter. You want to go to London, don't you, girls?'

Leonora and Maria flung themselves into his arms and turned to regard their Mama with disapprobation. Thrown into confusion by this united front, she murmured and clucked, and said finally that as long as no one came to hear it, particularly her papa, she must admit to being deeply grateful.

Since Lord Trenchard was in his seventy-eighth year, and deaf into the bargain, the others felt that there was a reasonable chance of it escaping his notice. Once Lady Constance was convinced that their reprehensible association with trade was unlikely to become public property, apart from murmuring occasionally, 'As long as the patronesses of Almacks don't come to hear of it, for that would be *fatal,*' she allowed herself to view it with a more cheerful frame of mind.

Leonora, meanwhile, had been pondering the gist of Mr. Revell's announcement in a more practical spirit. With the fortunate discovery of deposits of coal on a small Midlands estate, Mr. Revell had conceived the notion of buying up a mill in the north, converting to power looms, and transporting his own fuel directly to it up the new canals. She said, 'Papa, do you still own the mill?'

'No,' Mr. Revell said, eyeing his daughter in fascination. 'I was doubtful of their future now the war is over. I've bought up the land round here again.'

'And coal is perfectly respectable,' Leonora persisted. 'I mean, no one is likely to become a social outcast for selling coal if it happens to be on their land.'

Even Lady Constance admitted this to be true.

'So there is our story!' Leonora said triumphantly. Kissing Mr. Revell exuberantly, she announced her intention of flinging away her brown pelisse. Her feelings about this garment had threatened to become obsessive ever since she had seen one of the maids from the nearby Hall wearing a blue merino one with three capes. It had the new puffed sleeves and reached down over the hands, and Leonora felt quite ill with envy when she thought of Druscilla casually bestowing it upon her maid.

'Though with a figure and complexion like hers,' she commented waspishly to Maria at the time, 'it must be *most* difficult to dress to advantage.'

Due to a mutual antagonism, Druscilla rarely invited her to the Hall, but Maria was a more frequent visitor. She had been privileged on occasions to leaf through the *Ladies' Magazine* and *La Belle Assemblée,* and Leonora now demanded that she should sketch out as many of the modes as she could recall, while Lady Constance questioned Mr. Revell on whether their new affluence would support the hiring of a house.

The discussion lasted through dinner, but it was finally decided that they should all go up to town and lodge in an hotel so that they could look over the dwellings available, and procure a new wardrobe for themselves. On the question of servants, Leonora and Maria were as one in refusing to take Betty on the threefold grounds that she was inefficient, she sniffed, and she had a tendency towards hysterics in the slightest emergency.

'Besides carrying on with the groom,' Leonora added, to clinch it.

Lady Constance stared at her, scandalised, and wondered uneasily whether Leonora's conduct was likely to meet with approval of the high-bred dames who led the fashionable world.

Maria roused no such worries. Though quiet and shy, she was undoubtedly a beauty. Her pansy-brown eyes, with their curling lashes, were bound to make an instant appeal, and she was possessed of a perfect complexion and fairy-like figure. Both girls also were fashionably dark, with their ringlets at the moment tied up in a Clytie knot.

Viewing Leonora, even through a mother's eyes, Lady Constance was less hopeful. True, she had a pair of amber eyes of rare beauty, and a complexion as clear as Maria's, but the rest of her features were unremarkable, and she was disastrously tall. She was also over-inclined to speak her mind; a thing that Lady Constance and a succession of harassed governesses had tried, in vain, to correct. With only a very modest dowry, Leonora was going to be more difficult to get off.

However, there were more immediate worries, and Lady Constance, distractedly thinking back to her prosperous youth, trusted that things had not changed too much since she last had the management of a large household.

Then there was the delicate matter of how to approach her sister. Lady Margaret lived in high style in London, a formidable member of the *ton,* and for years the arrival of one of her letters had brought on a severe bout of depression. Her own two daughters had made excellent marriages, and Lady Constance felt that if she had a spark of sisterly feeling, she would have offered to sponsor her less fortunate nieces into society. The offer was never made, and Lady Constance could not bring herself to suggest it. In her more honest moments she admitted to herself that in spite of everything, she was really happy with Edmund, and would not exchange her own life for all the fortune at her sister's command if it also entailed a husband who indulged in notorious *affaires,* and had created an unbroken series of scandals, almost from the day of the wedding.

Lady Margaret's goodwill, however, was vitally important in this venture. She had the entry and connections which Lady Constance, in her straitened circumstances, had been forced to let lapse over the years. It was of no use to carry the girls off to London unless they received invitations from the right quarters.

In the end she decided to write a conciliatory letter, a composition calculated to arouse interest and soothe any qualms the tight-fisted Lady Margaret might feel about being involved in expense.

Once it was sealed and despatched, she sighed with relief, and turned to other matters of paramount importance. They all had their hair fashioned in the latest styles, and laid the foundations of their wardrobe; Leonora, with what Lady Constance felt to be unnecessary violence, making a bonfire of her brown pelisse and various other items of clothing for which she had developed an undying hatred. She watched with satisfaction until they had burned to the last thread, stating that she could now be on equal terms with the maids from the Hall. Her mama shuddered, and once more tried to instill into her the need for decorum.

'For in the beginning I am relying on your Aunt Margaret to get invitations for us, and I can assure you she would never endanger her own reputation if she thought you were likely to let her down. Neither of you are to be presented at court, but I am hopeful that she can get us admitted to Almack's. But, Leonora, you *must* be careful. It is so exclusive that you can be refused vouchers for the slightest thing!'

But Leonora said blithely that circumstances had forced her to be decorous for too long and since she was not beautiful, she had decided to be stylish. Unable to still the trepidation in her bosom, Lady Constance bore them off to London.

The manner of this, however, after so many years of economy, could not fail to bring its own satisfaction. The aged coach had been replaced by a travelling carriage, and Lady Constance was conscious of an inward glow as they swept up to the front door of their new home, Leonora slightly marring the occasion by saying, in strong local dialect, that she wished squire's daughter from the 'All could see them now. Since Lady Constance had a strong suspicion that this had been overheard by the superior butler and footman who were receiving them into the house, she was forced to quell a desire to box her ears.

By nightfall they were settled in, and awaiting dinner which was to be served at the later town hours, too tired to do anything except discuss their plans for the future.

Putting things in order of priority, it was decided that on the following day they should pay a morning call on Lady Margaret. Unfortunately, when morning arrived, Leonora's ambition to be dashing caused her to array herself in a vivid green walking dress that Lady Constance had been extremely doubtful about when it was made up, and would certainly not create the impression she hoped for on Lady Margaret. In a twitter of anxiety she ruthlessly dragged it over her head again, and Leonora eventually presented herself in a more sober shade of blue.

When they found themselves face to face with the aunt they had never seen, Leonora was strongly of the opinion that her mama had been over-scrupulous. Massive of bosom and hard of eye, Lady Margaret was dressed in the most ultra-modern style, and Leonora watched her in fascination, certain that she would ooze out of the top of her high-waisted gown before the visit was at an end.

She informed Maria in an undervoice that it was the most obscene spectacle she had ever witnessed, a remark that nearly caused Maria to lose control of herself, and she was only brought to order by a beseeching look from Lady Constance.

It was almost immediately obvious that Lady Margaret was disposed to be affable, and equally clear that she was determined to get to the root of their sudden change of fortune. Since coal was respectable, Lady Constance prattled on desperately, contriving to give the impression that it was so thick on the ground in Staffordshire that it was hardly necessary to do more than shovel it up. Never, even in her youth, a match for her formidable elder sister, she began to falter in her explanation, and Leonora boiled at her inability to halt the relentless inquisition.

At last, however, Lady Margaret appeared to be satisfied, and turned to make gracious conversation with her nieces. ('Making sure she didn't sponsor any dirty dishes,' Leonora commented afterwards.) Lancashire mills and wool were so firmly imprinted in Maria's mind that she was afraid to open her mouth in case the words slipped out of their own volition, so the burden of making responses fell almost entirely on Leonora. Incensed by the rudeness of her aunt's cross-examination, she adopted a simpering manner, and uttered two-edged remarks with every sentence, causing Lady Constance, seated opposite, to clutch her reticule in a state of acute fright.

A reference to the immodesty of modern styles made her reach for her salts, while Leonora, her amber eyes opened wide, assured her aunt that she had seen dresses without so much as a shift beneath them. This was the wildest prevarication, since Leonora, in the fastness of Revell House, had never had the opportunity of witnessing any such thing. Lady Constance closed her eyes, and devoutly hoped that her sister would never see Leonora in the white-spangled gown she had ordered on their last shopping expedition.

But in spite of everything the visit was a success. Lady Margaret, totally unacquainted with Leonora, could not perceive anything unusual in her manner, and her self-esteem was too great to allow of her taking Leonora's ambiguous remarks at any other than their face value.

She was charmed to have met them at last, and they must come to the evening party she was giving the following week. She even promised to have a word or two with Lady Jersey about their vouchers for Almack's. Lady Constance was able to feel that everything she set out to do had been successfully accomplished.

'Not that my nerves weren't stretched to the limit,' she informed Leonora, as they paraded determinedly round Hyde Park that afternoon.

Unrepentant, Leonora said, 'She wouldn't notice anything. And once she has presented us at her party, she can't very well change her mind without looking foolish.' She chuckled. 'Did you ever see anything like her dress! I expected to find her encased in purple satin. I swear she nearly fell out of the top of it when she sat down next to us.'

Lady Constance glanced round sharply to see if Maria was listening, but her younger daughter was totally absorbed in the scene around her. She had a slightly wistful air, and Leonora admitted to a twinge herself. London was all she hoped, but her daydreams had conveniently skipped over this friendless, awkward stage. In her winter evening reveries she had been transformed straight to the glittering ballrooms, where, exquisitely gowned, she was eagerly solicited to dance by gentlemen of rank and address.

She felt a little raw and countrified. At home, no matter what their circumstances, she had been Miss Revell of Revell House. Here, no one knew her name or her face.

True, one or two people had turned to look at them, including one gentleman, who, by the height of his shirt collar and the complexity of his neckcloth, she presumed to be one of the dandy set. He had found it necessary to assist his gaze by the use of his quizzing glass, and Leonora glanced at her mama to see what she made of it.

She suffered a surprise. The flustered chatelaine of Revell House was once more the Lady Constance Winton, daughter of Lord Trenchard. Assurance flowed from her as she directed a quelling stare at the gentleman who was impeding their progress, and Leonora was conscious of a new respect as he stepped aside with a slight bow.

She whispered 'Bravo!' but Lady Constance merely tutted, and said:

'Well, you would wear that green walking dress, in spite of what I told you.'

There was only one incident in their walk, when Lady Constance, a trifle pink with pleasure, recognised a friend from her girlhood. They exchanged married names and addresses, and Mrs. Partington asked if Leonora and Maria rode in the park as her own daughters frequently did. They parted with mutual promises to visit, and this small occurrence made them all feel more at ease.

They stayed at home in the evening. Mr. Revell was not arriving until the following day, and without a gentleman to escort them they could not visit any of the public amusements.

Leonora deplored their lack of a personable male, and played the pianoforte, at which she was remarkably proficient, due both to a natural flair and the fact that their previous mode of life had afforded long hours in which to practise.

At the other end of the room Lady Constance busied herself with putting into some sort of order the profusion of letters, bills, and jottings with which the writing-table drawer was already half full. These were in wild confusion, ranging from the wages paid to the abigail to a reminder that she needed slippers to go with a certain ball gown.

'Good gracious! And we've scarce been here a day! Leonora, if you should be asked to play at any time, that last piece would be just the thing, but whatever happens, don't, I implore you, let anyone prevail upon you to sing. Which reminds me, I was so put about when we went to visit your aunt that I quite forgot to ask her about a dancing master. I shall have to call on her again.' She paused, slightly dampened by the prospect, and Leonora, who had embarked on the sonatina a second time, stopped with a crashing chord.

'Heavens! We can't dance properly, and I never even thought of it!' The visions of glittering ballrooms receded even further. 'What about Aunt Margaret's party?'

'There won't be dancing. I checked on the invitation,' Lady Constance assured her, busily conning her lists again. 'Music and cards. You might find it rather dull, but there are bound to be some invitations arising from it and you must be prepared in time.'

The party became the focal point of their lives. The days were filled pleasantly enough with visiting the shops and circulating libraries, and Mr. Revell, on his arrival, took them to the theatre, but without Lady Margaret they lacked the entrée to the evening entertainments.

Even Leonora admitted to a slight feeling of nervousness when the day arrived, and when they were actually getting themselves ready Lady Constance found herself fluttering from room to room like an agitated hen, fearful of some unforeseen calamity. But in the end they were completed in time and presented themselves for inspection.

She felt the tears start to her eyes as she surveyed Maria. Dressed all in white, as became her eighteen years, the absence of colour, so fatal on some girls, brought out her clear complexion and the delicate pink of her cheeks. The deceptively plain gown was embroidered in silver round the hem, and across her arms she carried a silver shawl, its narrowing ends reaching almost to the ground. Lady Constance had banned any jewellery except for the pearl drops in her ears, and her maid had woven artificial flowers into her hair, so that they were half hidden by the dark tresses. She was delicate and fairylike, and Lady Constance was forced to dab the moisture from her eyes.

Leonora did not arouse the same protective instincts, but arrayed for the first time in the full glory of evening dress she was certainly impressive. She had overborne her mama's desire to present her in simple white, declaring that at nearly twenty-one she was past it. Instead she was dressed in her favourite shade of amber; a rich satin, appliqued round the neck and hem, and once more against Lady Constance's advice, had dressed her hair on the top of her head. Her mama admitted that she looked regal and elegant, but privately hoped that there would not be a superabundance of short men at the party.

She kissed them both, and fluttered away to make sure that Mr. Revell and the recently arrived and extremely reluctant Simon were not going to cause delay.

The short journey in the coach giving her time to collect her scattered thoughts, she emerged at the other end with stately calm and an autocratic tilt to her turban. Whatever her private flusters, her public manner commanded Leonora's admiration. Following in the wake of the silks and gauzes and muslins ascending the stairs, she was conscious of a distinct feeling of trepidation in the pit of her stomach, but Lady Margaret's blatant hypocrisy as she kissed her cheek in greeting did much to restore the balance of her feelings.

They eased themselves into the already overcrowded drawing room, and Lady Constance steered them to a sofa. 'We must wait until your aunt is free to make some introductions,' she whispered. 'Maria, don't play with your fringe!'

Maria dropped the fringe of her shawl and clutched her reticule instead, and Leonora assumed a cool smile and leaned back to watch the gathering through a strategically placed potted palm.

She was dwelling with interest on a young woman with long teeth and a languid air when she was enveloped in an aroma of lavender, and found herself gazing into Lady Margeret's grey satin bosom.

Startled, she rose to her feet, and found she was being introduced to Lady Jersey. The patroness of Almack's was known to her by name and reputation, and she looked round desperately for Lady Constance. Somehow, she had been detached from them, and Maria, sinking into a curtsey beside her, seemed to have been struck dumb.

It was left to herself to make the proper responses, but her conversational powers were not unduly strained. Lady Jersey, her bright, intelligent eyes darting everywhere, chattered incessantly, then, quite suddenly, leaving a half-heard remark trailing in the air, she was gone. Leonora turned indignantly on Maria.

'A fine help you were!'

'As soon as I realised who she was I couldn't think of a word to say.'

'That was obvious to both of us,' Leonora returned tartly.

Before Maria could defend herself their aunt was upon them again, all smiles and teeth.

'Dear Lady Jersey. I know your mama was most anxious for you to meet her. Well, we have quite a little group of young people here tonight, so I must make some of them known to you.'

She swept down the room, clearing a path by her sheer presence, and they were left to scurry in her wake like royal attendants.

'I hope the leg of her draws drops off,' Leonora muttered venomously. 'Introducing the country cousins.' She mimicked Lady Margaret's over-refined accents. 'Charming girls, of course, but terribly green. We must do our best to make them feel at home.'

Maria cast her a scared glance, and Lady Margaret, having adroitly gathered up a number of people from along her route, began introductions. Half the names passed over Leonora's head, and she gave up trying to remember the faces that went with them.

'Miss Harford, the daughter of one of my very oldest friends,' her aunt was saying. 'And this is Mr. Rochford. Mr. Rochford, I know I can leave you to procure some refreshment for my nieces. They are new to our town ways, you know.'

'And the methods of procuring refreshments are so *very* different in the country,' Leonora said limpidly.

She found she was wasting her breath: Mr. Rochford

was not attending. With half-open mouth he was staring at Maria's delicately flushed countenance, while she, a bemused expression on her face, gazed back. The silence deepened, and Leonora watched with interest, her first revelation of love at first sight. It was an affecting spectacle, and she was loth to break it up, but Miss Harford, the only other witness to the scene, was visibly stiffening with indignation. For Mr. Rochford, so long impervious to her beauty, charm and wit, to sink, in her presence, under the spell of a naive provincial was a severe blow to her self-esteem.

Taking the situation all round, Leonora deemed it time to call them back to earth. She pointedly confessed to a thirst, whereupon Mr. Rochford, called to a sense of his obligations, departed in search of lemonade. Leonora studied him afresh as he crossed the room. Not even the high-flown romances with which she beguiled herself at Revell House had prepared her for the drama which had just taken place, but even so brief a study of the participants convinced her that they were both thoroughly smitten.

She debated slipping away in search of Lady Constance to discover such interesting facts as his background and eligibility, but it would mean leaving Maria to Miss Harford's tender mercies, and the beauty was glittering dangerously. Besides, she could not imagine her aunt having anyone in her drawing room who was not socially acceptable.

Mr. Rochford returned, guiding a waiter who bore a trayload of delicacies, and she watched indulgently as he and Maria were reunited over a plate of route cakes. Since he appeared to be almost totally inarticulate, she felt they would suit very well, but for herself she preferred her conversation more stimulating. Murmuring an excuse which went unheeded, she slipped away to find mama and acquaint her with the interesting situation.

'Mr. Rochford!' Lady Constance exclaimed. 'He must be a son of Mary Webberly. I remember she married a Rochford.' She had been enjoying a comfortable chat with a woman, who, it turned out, had been presented in the same season as herself, and all the old names and half-forgotten recollections were flooding back. 'She was more a friend of your aunt's, but I recall her very well. I must have a word with Margaret about him.' She moved purposefully away, majestic in her role of chaperone, and Leonora followed. To her mind, Mr. Rochford did not present the appearance of a dangerous rake, and she was of the opinion that the affair needed delicate nurturing.

Mr. Rochford, however, successfully overcame his natural cowardice and presented himself on their doorstep the following morning. He took Maria driving in the park, and feeling that this was pointed enough to call for immediate investigation, Lady Constance set out at once to inform her sister.

She came back bearing heartening tidings. Lady Margaret gave the most comfortable account of his character, and also confided that Mrs. Rochford had begun to despair of his ever showing any interest in the fair sex. Compared with his previous attitude, for him to take Maria driving practically amounted to a declaration.

And Mr. Rochford continued to appear with pleasing regularity. He came with offerings of flowers, bashfully bestowed, and invitations to various entertainments which included all the ladies.

Simon, forever meeting him on the steps, or stopping to chat with him in the hall, thought him an excellent fellow, but it was not until Mr. Rochford took him to a cock-fight that it occurred to him that in squiring a young man several years his junior he was showing an uncommon interest in the family. Since he was not observant, he was forced to seek enlightenment as to which of his sisters was drawing Mr. Rochford so constantly to the house.

Lady Constance confessed that they cherished hopes for Maria. Her first rush of gratification having abated a little, her ever present terror now was that Mr. Rochford might discover their lamentable association with trade.

'For his mother is as starched up as your Aunt Margaret, and I live in fear and dread of her getting a whisper of it. Not that there is much she could do after sponsoring the girls without making herself look ridiculous, and that she would never do, as well as being so closely related.' Slightly breathless, she paused, and Simon assured her that he had no intention of blighting his sister's hopes. He made his escape, and informed Leonora later that their mother was becoming a regular natterbox.

'She always has been,' Leonora said dispassionately, 'only you're never at home to notice.'

'I'm not surprised that Maria seems likely to get herself off before you,' he retorted, stung. 'I say, Mama seems pretty certain of it, doesn't she?'

'He is escorting us to Almack's tonight, and we have it on Aunt Margaret's infallible authority that he has never set foot in the place before!'

'Well, he seems a good sort of fellow. Beats me why he should want to marry Maria. I like him better than that Finchley who was dangling after you, in any event. Saw him this morning, by the way. He was with the copper-headed female.'

Leonora also saw him when they attended Almack's. Their introduction to this high spot of society had been delayed until they were proficient enough with their dancing, and Maria, on Mr. Rochford's arm, looked forward to the evening with blissful expectancy.

Lining the wall with the other damsels, Leonora viewed it with mixed feelings. Her feet itched to join in the dancing, but sometimes these social evenings seemed oddly flat. She admitted to herself that she had not taken like Maria. Gentlemen did not rush forward to beg for the honour of a dance with a partner who was likely to top them by several inches, and, more critical than her sister, she did not make friends with the same ease. Maria already had a host of friends with whom she could pass a pleasant hour, but Leonora found herself unable to utter the inanities that passed for conversation at these gatherings.

Watching her with Mr. Rochford, she was honestly delighted that they should have fallen in love, but she could not discover anything in him to make her own heart flutter in her breast.

Interrupting her self-analysis, her aunt and Lady Jersey bore down on her, and she rose to her feet.

Lady Jersey smiled on her. 'My dear, your first visit to us. I must introduce you to some of the others as soon as this dance is finished.' Then, apparently dismissing Leonora from her mind, she settled down to talk to Lady Margaret, and Leonora, who had always had a lamentable tendency towards eavesdropping, caught a reference to Catherine Harford, and stretched her ears.

Lady Jersey's laugh trilled out. 'My dear, whatever the others say, I wouldn't dream of refusing her a voucher. I declare it's as good as a play to watch her trying to play off Everard and Finchley. Though, mark you, I think she'll lose Finchley if she's not careful. Everard is making her the talk of the town. I hold the mother as much to blame, of course.'

With this information to give added interest, Leonora viewed Catherine and Sir Mark with keener appreciation. She had given Sir Mark a civil bow when they first arrived, but it was obvious that he barely recollected her. No one existed for him but the lovely Catherine. Certainly if there was anyone capable of eclipsing Maria, it was the red-head. There was not a freckle to mar the perfection of her skin, and the flutter of her lashes as her large grey eyes looked meltingly into Sir Mark's was an art in itself. Leonora made a mental note to copy it, since it was the only field in which she could reasonably hope to compete.

She looked round to see if she could guess which was Lord Everard. She had not spent considerable time in Mr. Rochford's company without learning something of his closest friend, and he was supposed to be present tonight.

She heard her name spoken, and realised that Mr. Rochford was standing by her, accompanied by another man. Rising from her hurried curtsey, her eyes travelled up what must surely have been the tallest man in the room, and came to rest on a wing of silver hair.

For the first time in her life, her heart gave an uncomfortable lurch, but she managed to say, quite distinctly, 'I think Lord Everard and I have met before!'

4

He frowned in puzzlement and an imp of malice possessed her.

'Last autumn,' she said helpfully. 'But we only met very briefly. In fact we were never properly introduced.'

The corners of his mouth twitched appreciatively, and she went on: 'It was all so confusing. My maid was in hysterics, and I recall that you were having trouble with your horse. I know I didn't catch your name myself!' She flashed a smile at the perplexed Mr. Rochford. 'When you spoke of Lord Everard, of course I never connected the two!'

'Of course,' the earl echoed. 'And when Paul spoke of Miss Revell I never connected it with *you*. May we renew our acquaintance on the floor?'

Leonora glanced at him uncertainly, aware that she had lost the initiative somewhere, but he was holding out his arm, so she placed her hand on it and they made their way to where the sets were forming.

She risked a quick glance at his face. He was watching her with amusement, and said provocatively, 'It was dark too. In fact, considering all the circumstances, Miss Revell, I am flattered by your recognition.'

Leonora took a deep breath. This cool nobleman, attired in the formal dress demanded at Almack's, seemed far removed from the moonlit road in Surrey. Her eyes went briefly back to the wing of silver. 'It was because of your . . .' she began, then froze. Over Lord Everard's shoulder she could see Sir Mark. He was glaring at the earl's back with undisguised hostility.

'Mark Finchley!' she breathed.

'A piquant situation,' the earl commented, without any visible signs of fright. 'But we meet quite frequently. His animosity is rooted in a different cause.'

He studied her consideringly. 'Did you ever feel impelled to discuss our previous meeting with him?'

'No,' Leonora said nervously. She felt strongly that a more private spot would be better suited to such a dangerous conversation.

'And do you feel obliged to mention it to him in the future?'

'We seldom meet nowadays,' Leonora replied. She was answering almost at random, very much aware of the people close to them in the set. Anyone who cared to listen might hear what they were saying.

She realised as soon as she had spoken that Lord Everard might think that she had given a deliberately evasive reply, but the opening bars of the dance had struck up, and speech, for the moment, was impossible. Besides, the whole of her concentration was needed to remember the steps.

The music ended, and, flushed and exhilarated, she returned on the earl's arm to where Maria was smiling radiantly up at Mr. Rochford.

Still very conscious of their unfinished conversation, she glanced hesitantly up at the earl, wondering if he would reopen the subject, but his expression was enigmatic. He indicated the couple with a nod of his head, and said, 'When do the wedding bells ring out?'

'He hasn't yet made her an offer,' Leonora returned absently, her thoughts still in a whirl. He would surely not suppose that she intended to betray the best friend of her future brother-in-law! 'Papa says if he's going to, he hopes it will be before next Wednesday, because he's got to go north on . . .' Her voice trailed away, and she bit her lip. She had so nearly made a reference to Lady Constance's dreaded mill. Though if it came to guilty secrets, she thought indignantly, association with trade hardly came into the same class as highway robbery.

There was a questioning lift to his eyebrows, and she said lamely, 'On a visit. And I should have thought that you were probably more aware of Mr. Rochford's intentions than I, Lord Everard.'

'Attack is always the best form of defence,' he said approvingly. He led her to a vacant chair, and bowed to Lady Constance. 'We must find an opportunity of continuing our discussion, Miss Revell.' A further bow and he was gone, and the next time Leonora saw him he was dancing with Catherine Harford, who glittered like the crystal chandeliers. Her vivid face smiled up at him, and something she said made him burst out laughing.

Suddenly Leonora felt inadequate and insipid, and almost wished she were back at Revell House.

Mr. Rochford, meeting the earl by appointment three days later, was not wearing his normally insouciant expression. Two things had occurred to disturb him, and he mulled over which to mention first, while the earl rode patiently alongside. Lord Everard's big black gelding, less tolerant, tried the efficaciousness of a stiff-legged buck, and Mr. Rochford was momentarily diverted.

'I wish you'd keep your distance with that brute,' he complained, gathering up his own chestnut.

'You shouldn't ride with a slack rein!'

Mr. Rochford grunted, and decided to take the plunge with the less serious problem. 'Your cousin's widow's back in town!'

'Confound the woman,' the earl said feelingly. 'Why couldn't she wait another few weeks and make it a decent six months. What's she up to this time?'

Mr. Rochford rubbed the end of his nose. 'Well, nothing,' he said, anxious to be fair. 'Except that I'd say from the size of the house that she ain't living on what your cousin left her.'

'Digby! And is my ward with her?'

Mr. Rochford nodded. 'Not at all the thing to be going to parties already. Wearing colours too.'

'Well, she can't be causing too much of a stir if it hasn't reached my ears.'

'Lot of disapproval,' Mr. Rochford said, 'but not actual scandal so far. Lack of evidence,' he opined sagely.

'I wish she'd conduct her *affaires* abroad. She'll never get Sarah married off unless I dower her with a fortune.' He saw that Mr. Rochford's gloomy expression had not lightened. 'What else?'

Mr. Rochford took a deep breath. 'Been a bit of talk in the clubs in the last few days. Finchley was in his cups, apparently, and set it about that you were the Black Gentleman. Told one of his toadies that he's seen where he put the bullet through your arm. Must have been after that day at Jackson's.'

'I wondered if he might,' the earl said slowly.

'Ain't you worried?'

'By Finchley's unsupported word?' The earl shook his head. 'No. He's made such a fool of himself recently over Catherine Harford, I think it will be taken along with all the rest.'

'If you'd stop chasing that redhead, there wouldn't be any more trouble,' Mr. Rochford said irritably. 'If she can't have you and your title, she wants Finchley's money. Put her out of her misery and we'll all have some peace.'

'How do you know my intentions aren't honourable?' the earl said, giving way to an ignoble impulse.

Mr. Rochford was incredulous. 'You never mean to marry the girl! She's only out for the best catch she can get on the market!'

'So are all the others,' the earl said, with assumed cynicism. 'Catherine Harford at least has the advantage of being the most decorative.'

'You'll end up fighting a duel with Finchley, and even if you don't, if you irritate him any more, he's not going to keep his mouth shut. What if he jogs a few memories and someone else recognises you?'

'Too late!' the earl said with a grin. 'Someone already has!'

He sent the black into a canter, and Mr. Rochford stared after him aghast, then spurred his chestnut on. The mare reared indignantly. Out of breath, and clutching his hat, he caught up with the earl and gasped out, 'Who?'

The earl took pity and reined back to a walk. 'Your little Maria's sister.'

Mr. Rochford's mouth dropped open. 'You don't mean to tell me you held her up!'

'Last autumn,' the earl said with a reflective smile. 'I couldn't think for a moment the other day why her face was familiar.'

'Well, you'd best forget the Harford chit and marry her! She's a bit too sharp for my taste, but if you have two of them blabbing it round the town, someone's bound to take them seriously. How did she find out?'

'I'm not sure. It was her coach I was holding up when Finchley's shot got me. She was just about to tell me at Almack's when he appeared on the scene. I must find out.'

'Marry her first and find out afterwards,' Mr. Rochford advised. 'Got a mind of her own, that girl.'

'Yes,' the earl said pensively. 'I rather gathered as much.' Casting his mind back, he clearly recalled her face at the window of the ancient coach. She had said something about having nothing of value, and his being welcome to her artificial flowers. In contrast, he remembered the elegant picture she had presented when he met her at the assembly.

'What do you know about the family?' he asked.

'Made a few enquiries,' Mr. Rochford admitted. 'My mother would kick up a fuss if she didn't like the background. Lady C's all right—old Trenchard's daughter, and the father's known in all the clubs. Don't know about money, but I ain't hanging out for a portion.'

'Has there been a sudden upswing in their fortunes?'

'Why? Something smoky?'

'Just an impression.' He set the black into a canter again. 'When are you making your formal application for Maria's hand?'

'What's it got to do with you?' Mr. Rochford said, with the belligerence of long friendship.

'Nothing,' the earl said cheerfully. 'Only you'd better make it before next Wednesday. Her father's going north. On a visit!'

Spurred on by the earl's disclosure, Mr. Rochford decided to call on his Maria's father the following morning. The faithful Brookes, who had his own means of discovering what went on in the world, was obliged to help him in and out of three coats before Mr. Rochford made his final choice. Smoothing the set of the shoulders with an indulgent hand, Brookes remarked knowingly that it was a fine enough day to walk such a short distance, and was gratified by the hunted look that overspread Mr. Rochford's countenance.

'Soon be over now, sir!' He gave a final expert flick with the brush, and stood back, satisfied that Mr. Rochford presented the appearance of the perfect gentleman.

Mr. Rochford, with no more excuse for dallying, picked up his cane and went out. His Maria was waiting for him to approach her father, and Lady Constance's relaxed and informal manners indicated that she considered the matter as good as settled.

Nevertheless, his footsteps took him twice past the house before he could nerve himself to ascend the front steps. The footman who opened the door, and who now permitted himself a small smile of welcome, afforded him a temporary means of escape. Informing Mr. Rochford that he rather thought the young ladies were in the front saloon, he prepared to lead the way, but the unhappy suitor, overcoming his craven impulses, announced that it was Mr. Revell he wished to see.

Encountering the same knowing smile that had characterised Brookes, Mr. Rochford swallowed, and was led into the study. Shaking Mr. Revell by the hand, he discovered that his carefully rehearsed speech had gone out of his head, and said desperately that it was a fine morning.

Mr. Revell agreed.

'Get some nasty showers in April,' Mr. Rochford went on.

Mr. Revell, his eyebrows twitching with mirth, agreed that you could get some very nasty showers in April. To ease his troubled visitor, he suggested a glass of sherry, and silence reigned until the footman brought in the decanter and glasses.

Pouring out with a liberal hand, Mr. Revell decided to help.

'I take it,' he said, perching comfortably on the desk, 'that you have come to see me concerning my younger daughter.'

Relieved, Mr. Rochford nodded, but remained silent.

Rapidly coming to the conclusion that he was going to have to make the proposal himself, Mr. Revell said, 'I realise that this is an affair of some delicacy. Can it be that you perhaps wish to marry my younger daughter?'

'That's it,' Mr. Rochford agreed, happy to find it so easily over.

'In that case, you have my permission. Drink your sherry.'

Beaming at his future father-in-law, Mr. Rochford obeyed, and confessed that he had never been so frightened in his life. 'Pop the notice in the paper now, and it's all done,' he said happily.

Mr. Revell viewed him consideringly. 'Told your parents what you intended yet?'

He met with a blank stare.

'Write and tell them first.' He submitted to having his hand gratefully pumped, and informed him tolerantly that Maria would be expecting him upstairs, then sat back behind his desk, waiting for the moment when he could enjoy a hearty laugh.

Mr. Rochford, having got the dread moment over, was now in that beatific state where he was convinced that all men, to be happy, must be married.

Bowing over Maria's hand with rare grace, he said proudly, 'Done it!' It then occurred to him that he was now officially engaged, and he leaned over and kissed her cheek.

Maria's eyes glowed. 'You actually asked Papa?'

'Yes . . . well . . .' Mr. Rochford temporised. 'He seemed to know what I'd come about. Everyone seemed to know what I'd come about,' he added, recalling the fatherly attitudes of Brookes and the footman. 'Everard was asking me about it the other day as well. Time he was getting married as well. Must be thirty by now.'

Leonora, waiting to wish the couple happy before slipping discreetly away, looked up quickly. A small knot seemed to have formed in her throat. 'Is Lord Everard contemplating matrimony then?'

'Seems to be,' Mr. Rochford said. 'Mind you,' he continued gloomily, 'why, with all the females in London, he must choose . . . Not a friend of yours, is she?'

'Oh no,' Maria assured him. 'She hardly speaks to us. She seems so proud. But it often seems so with very beautiful girls.'

'Not all of 'em,' Mr. Rochford said, giving her an affectionate hug.

Simon, erupting into the room at that moment, took in the situation at a glance. 'Asked m'father, have you? Well, now you're in the family, there's something I've been meaning to ask you.' He took hold of Mr. Rochford's lapel as he spoke, and Mr. Rochford watched him with starting eyes.

'No,' he said firmly, removing the offending hand. Whatever his natural diffidence with the fair sex, he was perfectly capable of dealing with their brothers.

'I ain't even asked you yet!'

'Well, you're not driving my chestnuts!'

'That wasn't it.'

'Wasn't it?' Mr. Rochford said, relieved.

'I wanted you to put me up for Whites!'

'Ask your father,' Mr. Rochford said promptly.

Simon considered for a moment. 'I could, I suppose. Then you could second me.'

'Wouldn't second anybody in a waistcoat like that,' Mr. Rochford returned stolidly. 'Got my reputation to consider.'

'Oh.' Simon eyed him with dawning respect. 'Well, you can come with me to look at a horse this afternoon.'

'No, I can't. We're going to buy the ring.'

'You've engaged yourself to a very disobliging fellow,' Simon told Maria.

Leonora laughed. 'We should be grateful if you could

take him somewhere where he would acquire a little more polish.'

'I could take him round some of the *ton* parties,' Mr. Rochford offered. 'Brush up his card-playing and improve his manners. Could introduce him to some eligible girls too, if you want to get rid of him.'

Simon was so keenly interested in girls that Lady Constance worried when she thought about it, but they were not of the type likely to be present at any of the parties Mr. Rochford attended. He gave his future brother-in-law a swift grin and declined his well meant offer. True, his faith in women had been severely tried the previous week, when his ardour, successfully surviving a confrontation with a rival on the stairs of his lady's lodgings, had been extinguished without a flicker when he discovered her the following evening with a head full of curl papers. However, almost immediately afterwards, he had had a most encouraging encounter with a little blonde.

Mr. Rochford regarded him with faint disapproval. Aware of some of his more riotous exploits, he read his mind with an ease that would have astonished the graceless Simon. But he was three and twenty, and Mr. Rochford decided that it was no business of his, and, turning his attention back to the girls, nobly suggested a ride.

Leonora hesitated. Her hack was newly purchased, and she had not yet had an opportunity to try it out. On the other hand, she felt the engaged couple deserved a little privacy.

Mr. Rochford settled it by pointing out that he was already in breeches and topboots, and it was the work of a moment to send round for his own hack. Weakly, she agreed, and went up to change into her new velvet riding habit. Mr. Rochford had to learn sometime that Maria, whom he was going to take for better or worse, was, to put it kindly, an indifferent rider.

Waiting in the front saloon, she knew Mr. Rochford had an inkling of what was to come as soon as he laid eyes on the sedate little hack. Her own mount was sidling and flinging up his head, and Mr. Rochford cravenly suggested that they should bring the groom as well.

'I won't disgrace you by falling off,' Leonora promised comfortingly.

Eyeing her horse doubtfully, Mr. Rochford said, 'Might not have any choice in the matter.' Since the animal would not stand still, he threw her into the saddle while the groom held its head. He felt sure that somewhere there must be a happy medium between this jittery grey and Maria's little bay, which he strongly suspected of being a slug.

Unperturbed, Leonora placed the skirts of her habit and ordered the groom to let go his head. Immediately, the grey swung in half-circle and made for the mews, but Leonora swiftly turned him back and touched him with her whip. He responded by humping up his back, and Mr. Rochford wished desperately that he had suggested a walk.

Leonora brought him up alongside and said calmly, 'I don't think he's really nappy. I should say he's been badly ridden, and, of course, he hasn't been out of the stable since he arrived.'

It was then discovered that Maria's mount would not budge until someone gave him a lead. Obviously, Mr.

Rochford was beginning to think poorly of Mr. Revell as a judge of horseflesh, and Leonora was torn between allowing him to continue in his false impression, and informing him that his beloved was one of those doubtful equestriennes who could not be brought to sit on a horse unless it was guaranteed safe for a child of eight. Also, since Maria did not like to be situated too far from the ground, Mr. Rochford found he had to turn his head both backwards and downwards every time he wished to address a remark to her.

Appalled by the prospect of conveying them through the traffic to the park, he shepherded them along the road, and his worst fears were realised. Whilst Leonora appeared to have no difficulty in controlling the grey's desire to take off with her, he was by no means traffic proof. Between prodding along Maria's reluctant mount, and trying to be prepared for the grey's violent shys at street vendors and ladies' parasols, Mr. Rochford was beginning to break out in a nervous sweat.

When Lord Everard appeared from a side road, he greeted him with relief, and was not in the least offended by the earl's undisguised amusement.

'Trouble?' the earl murmured.

'Trouble!' Mr. Rochford echoed. 'One won't go and t'other won't stop!' Harassed, he looked back in time to see Leonora being carried into a lamp-post by a particularly violent shy. 'For God's sake look after that one for me!'

Laughing heartily, the earl reined back, and Leonora, her eyes watering from a painful knock on the knee, eyed him with resentment.

'Rejoicing in the misfortunes of others, my lord?'

Recalling Mr. Rochford's bedevilled expression, he confessed his guilt, thereby unwittingly increasing Leonora's hostility.

'He's surely not a very comfortable ride for you, Miss Revell.'

'I daresay he isn't at the moment,' Leonora said defiantly, 'but I prefer him to some livery stables hack.'

At that moment a piece of paper blew across the road and wrapped round the foreleg of the earl's long-tailed black. He reared up, and Leonora allowed a smug expression to settle over her countenance.

'I entirely agree with you,' the earl said. 'Let's hurry and get them into the park.'

'You won't be able to hurry,' Leonora told him maliciously. 'We have to wait for Trojan.'

Lord Everard turned in his saddle to watch the little bay.

'Can't Trojan go any faster?'

'It's my belief that he doesn't know how to canter!'

'In which case,' the earl said firmly, 'I hope your sense of propriety doesn't forbid our going a little way ahead, because I propose that we trot.'

In reply, Leonora gathered up her reins. The grey, when he was allowed to go, had a long, smooth stride, and Mr. Rochford and Maria were soon left far behind. They swept through the gates of the park and broke into a canter.

'That's better,' Leonora said with satisfaction, when they pulled them back to a walk. 'Papa has never chosen a bad one for me yet. Where do you think the others are?'

'I rather think we've lost them. You will have to be resigned to my sole company, and to be candid I think we shall do better without them.'

'Just because Maria is not a particularly good rider there is no need to sneer at her,' Leonora said defensively.

'Miss Revell, there are men who sail the seas purely for pleasure. In my opinion it is a wet and dangerous pastime, and I am not of their number. I do not despise Maria, but if you are trying to gammon me that it adds to your pleasure to have to keep pace with the admirable Trojan, I must tell you that I cannot believe you.'

'It doesn't,' Leonora admitted, 'but it smites my conscience to be forced to say so.'

'Very proper. And having settled that, I have a question to ask you. What made you so certain who I was when we met at Almack's? After all, on that first occasion it was dark and I was masked. I will tell you now that at the time I was very tempted to appear amazed and give you a setdown. I could have done, you know.'

'Why didn't you?' Leonora asked, a small feeling of hope beginning to form.

His next words dashed her utterly.

'I thought it might not successfully silence you!'

Leonora eyed him frostily. 'Lord Everard, you have a reputation for considerable address. I cannot imagine how you came by it!' To give relief to her feelings, she sent the grey into a fast canter, but the earl caught up with her within a few strides.

'One is only supposed to indulge in a decorous hand canter in the park, Miss Revell, and you still have not answered my question.'

'I should have thought your recollections would have been equal to mine,' Leonora said perversely. 'But, of course, I am forgetting. I had never been held up before, and I expect, to you, the incident was merely one of hundreds!'

The earl's lips twitched. 'That would be putting it too high, and I cannot previously recall any of my victims being large-minded enough to warn me that I was in imminent danger of being shot by their protector! I assure you that the incident does stick in my memory.'

Leonora felt a slow flush rise up her cheeks. Without looking up she knew that he was watching her. She said stiffly, 'I think we should try to find the others.'

For the rest of the ride, she refused to speak except in answer to a direct question, and took an impenitent pleasure in the fact that he was still none the wiser as to how she had recognised him. Since they did not meet up with Maria and Mr. Rochford on their way, Lord Everard escorted her home, and she prepared to bid him goodbye as distantly as good manners would allow. Unfortunately, in her haste to dismount before he could come to her assistance, she hooked her skirt over the pommel of the saddle, and was forced to hang there, rigid with mortification, until he lifted her to the ground. She gritted her teeth to thank him, then made the unwelcome discovery that her knee, while only slightly painful in the saddle, would not support her on the ground.

'I've a good mind to leave you to hop up the steps on your own,' the earl said, grinning openly. 'You would be well served for your gracious treatment of my conversational efforts. Can you walk on it at all?'

'Yes,' Leonora said baldly. Wild ideas of standing there until she could prevail upon some passer-by to pull the bell for her formed in her mind, but the earl frustrated them by remaining to see her into the house. 'No,' she corrected weakly, 'I can't,' and with a feeling closely akin to hatred, accepted the support of his proffered arm, and hopped inelegantly to the flagway. The poised and beautiful Miss Harford, she was certain, would never find herself in such a predicament, or if she did, the earl would probably carry her gallantly in, like some knight of old. The fact that if he had offered to do any such thing she would have refused him with loathing, she ignored. She felt that he should have offered. No doubt, if instead of five foot nine, she had been a fragile five foot three, he would have done, she thought dismally. She had no patience with men who could not see beyond an air of delicacy and a lovely face. But Catherine was by far too clever to show the unlikable side of her nature to a possible husband, and she felt mournfully that the discovery would come too late.

Depressed by these reflections, she thanked the earl in a small and quite charitable voice when she bade him good-bye, and was aided to her room by her abigail, where she spent half an hour rubbing liniment on her knee and brooding.

She was invaded then by Maria and Lady Constance. Maria had only just returned from her ride, and Lady Constance, due to the circumstances of having conceived the brilliant notion of giving an engagement party, had shut herself away in the small saloon. She had been busily working out the number of couples the modest ballroom would hold, and running over the little delicacies she would offer her guests, unaware that her elder daughter was lying injured above stairs. The butler, however, by tendering his sympathies, had combined the information with an announcement of luncheon, and Lady Constance rushed upstairs to ascertain the extent of the injuries.

She paused in the doorway.

'Good gracious! Whatever is that dreadful smell?'

'Liniment,' Leonora said dolefully.

'I've never smelled any like it before!'

'It's horse liniment,' Leonora explained.

Lady Constance shrieked. 'You've never been rubbing it on yourself!'

'Only my knee,' Leonora said, inspecting it. 'And it's improving already. My new grey took me into a lamppost.'

'We're due at Lady Netherby's tonight, and you can't go reeking of liniment!'

'If I hadn't put it on I shouldn't be able to go at all,' Leonora pointed out reasonably. She tried an experimental hop around the room. 'I should be all right as long as no one expects me to do a cotillion.'

'However did you get into the house?' Maria asked.

'That odious man had to help me,' Leonora said, unjustly imputing reluctance on Lord Everard's part. 'I'm sorry we left you behind, but the grey was pulling my arms out. I had the devil's own game to hold him.'

'Leonora!' Lady Constance said despairingly. Tardily, her brain fastened on to the first part of Leonora's speech. 'What odious man?'

'Lord Everard.'

'Leonora, what have you been about?' Lady Constance said, with suspicion. 'If you have offended him . . . Since Mr. Brummell has been discredited there's hardly a more influential man in London than Lord Everard, besides being Mr. Rochford's friend, and I'm sure he seemed a most pleasant man when I met him.'

'It was only about my horse,' Leonora fabricated lamely. She realised fully for the first time the seriousness of her private knowledge. It was certainly nothing she could share with her mother and Maria and she had no reason to suppose that Mr. Rochford knew of it either. She wondered if they hung you for being a highwayman when you were an earl, and decided that to get away with it you would need to be a duke or even the heir apparent.

She was still dwelling on the matter as she dressed, without enthusiasm, for Lady Netherby's ball. Normally she would have looked forward to an evening of dancing, but although she could manage to walk without a limp, clearly she would be unable to take the floor on this occasion. She began to coil her hair on top of her head, and pulled a face at herself in the mirror. Six months ago to attend a London ball had been the height of her ambitions and she was vaguely ashamed that she could feel discontented now that her dreams had been realised. Her silver-spangled gown gleamed in the candlelight; the pearls which had been Papa's Christmas gift glowed softly back from the mirror, and, feeling absurdly guilty, she slipped the matching drops through her ears.

On a sudden impulse she hunted through the drawers of her dressing table until she found the bunch of artificial flowers which used to adorn the hat she wore with the despised brown pelisse. Faintly dingy, its petals drooped pathetically, and she looked at it for a moment, then thrust it defiantly into the frame of the mirror. It would serve to remind her of the way Lady Constance worried over their future when they were buried at Revell House and of Papa's pleasure in being able to give them their London season.

Chastened by her reflections, she decided that the least she could do was to forget about highwaymen who were earls, and concentrate on fulfilling Lady Constance's dearest wish, which was to see both her daughters respectably married. Maria had already played her part and Leonora was uneasily aware of the proximity of her twenty-first birthday. Hostesses were inclined to usher her amongst the older girls, some of whom were in their third and even fourth season. Nightmarish visions arose of joining the sad ranks of those past hope, who took to wearing lace caps on their heads and chaperoned their juniors.

She shuddered, and mentally went through the men who had shown a glimmer of interest. While there were several, notably Mr. Denston, who would gravitate to her side at some point in an evening, and she was never short of someone to take her driving, there was only one man bowled over by her charms to the extent of inundating her with flowers, and he was totally ineligible. Daunted, she went over them again, wondering which could be lured on with a little encouragement, but the sad fact was that she liked none of them well enough to make the attempt.

'Come,' she told her reflection severely, 'you're no more than passably good-looking, and your dowry would hardly tempt a pauper. You cannot expect to compete for the pick of the season's catches; you will have to be satisfied with something considerably less than the best.' She pictured the persistent Mr. Eccleston, with his eternal nosegays, but no, she couldn't bring herself to sink as low as that. At one time she had no doubt that she could have secured Mark Finchley, who was a more important conquest than she had realised at the time, but whoever eventually journeyed to the altar with him was equally welcome. Her thoughts travelled on to Catherine Harford, who obviously did not despise Sir Mark as a possible husband, and, unbidden on its heels, there rose the vision of Lord Everard.

She sighed, and finally acknowledged the truth to herself. Wherever she was, and whoever she was with, the earl was there. His face would blot out the features of the man she was with; his tall figure would come before the form of the man she was dancing with. Mr. Denston was pleasant, easy company, and she had enjoyed herself enormously on their outings together, but his eyes did not narrow to slits of amusement when something appealed to his sense of humour. If their friendship ripened to something warmer, she had a strong suspicion that he would allow her to ride roughshod over his opinions and wishes, and she had a very poor idea of anyone who would let her have her own way when she was clearly in the wrong. He would never, like the earl, bring her up short with some pointed comment if he thought she was trying to be deliberately awkward. Mr. Denston wouldn't even think she could be awkward. It was a fault in herself that she was aware of, and she tried to overcome it, but it was there, and to her mind it was a poor sort of man who would condone it.

The earl did not condone it. He had the knack of making her feel unsophisticated and childish. She remembered that very morning, when in her hurry to do without his assistance she had caught herself on the saddle. And it served her right, she admitted. Anyone with a modicum of breeding and manners would never have got into such a situation. With a deepening melancholy, she realised that it had probably only been to oblige Mr. Rochford that he had escorted her. He was held to be one of the biggest flirts in London; there was not a debutante on the scene who did not hopefully encourage his slightest advance, so what on earth could he find to interest him in Leonora Revell, fresh from the country? The truth of the matter was that he didn't find anything at all. He was merely her future brother-in-law's friend, and she would be well advised to think of him as such, since she could not avoid meeting him frequently. He would probably be at Lady Netherby's tonight. It was one of the biggest events of the year so far, and it was proof positive of Lady Margaret's social pull that they had all been invited. Even Simon was attending with good grace.

Hopefully, she tried her knee once more, but it was unfit for anything but walking, and with unusually dampened spirits she picked up her velvet cloak and went to find Lady Constance.

They were a little late arriving, and she could hear the strains of a waltz as they entered, and the hiss of slippered feet sliding across the polished floor. It made her feel lower than ever. To sit down the side amongst the dowagers and dowdies was going to be torture. Apart from her natural love of dancing, she was held to be elegant and graceful on the floor, and knew she appeared to advantage.

Mr. Rochford led Maria away, Simon and her papa disappeared with some male acquaintances, and when Lady Constance once more discovered a long-lost friend of her youth she was bereft of company. Quelling her indignation at being so callously abandoned, she gazed round, trying to appear unconcerned, and saw Lord Everard strolling across the room towards her. She watched him warily, and he grinned down at her.

'May I have the honour of the next waltz, Miss Revell?'

His tone implied that she was sitting there because she lacked a partner, and, nettled, she said sharply, 'You, above all people, should know that I am unable to dance.'

He lowered himself beside her on the sofa, and said musingly, 'I wonder where you get your deplorable manners. Your mama seems the epitome of the graces, and I cannot think that she failed to bring up her daughters with a sense of what was proper. Though with Maria I find it difficult to judge. One can hardly commit many social solecisms if one remains almost entirely silent.'

Leonora's resolve to treat him with friendly reserve vanished. Raging, she retorted, 'If we're to talk of deplorable manners, I think mine will stand comparison with your own. That's the second time you have sneered at Maria in her absence!'

'I wasn't sneering,' the earl said mildly. 'I hold her uncommunicative manner to be a virtue. If half the females who have nothing to say would hold their tongues, we should be saved a deal of idle nonsense.' His eyes glinted down at her. 'You leap to conclusions too quickly. Like that grey of yours, you're headstrong.'

Leonora boiled over. 'He isn't headstrong! Merely because he's a little traffic shy . . .' The earl raised his brows in polite disbelief. 'I shall take him out before breakfast tomorrow when there isn't so much about.'

'An excellent idea. If you'd done that this morning, you'd have saved yourself an injured knee.'

Leonora gasped, but Lady Constance was approaching

and she was obliged to bottle her temper. The earl rose to his feet to greet her mama, then sauntered away.

Broodingly, Leonora watched him infiltrate himself into the group surrounding Catherine Harford and emerge with her on his arm a moment later. So he had simply been filling in his time until the beauty arrived!

In fact, she did the earl an injustice. Seeing her sitting alone, and somewhat forlorn, he had, with the most charitable of motives, gone to her assistance. Shrewdly suspecting that nothing would restore the tone of her mind more quickly than a little verbal battle, he had deliberately induced a mood of pugnacity, then, confident that it would carry her through the evening, left her to Lady Constance. Meanwhile, it afforded him considerable amusement to be able to detach Miss Harford from under the noses of half a dozen of her admirers. She was fluttering her lashes with a consummate artistry that evoked a dispassionate admiration in the earl. He had seen it practised on too many others to be unduly flattered, but if she wished to play games, he was very willing to oblige. He wondered where her sense of propriety would prompt her to stop, and with a casual remark about the insufferable heat of the ballroom, steered her out into the corridor.

Apparently he was still within her limits, for she merely said, 'And why are we come here, my lord?'

'In search of a little cool air. Don't you find the ballroom stifling?' He smiled at her, and glanced up and down the corridor. 'I don't think our hostess would object if we opened one of her windows.' He opened a door as he spoke, and held out his hand. By the readiness with which she whisked herself through, he deduced that it was not the first time that she had indulged in a little dalliance. She stationed herself under the light of the candle brackets, and the earl took the precaution of closing the curtains against any interested observers from the other side of the courtyard.

'Much cooler,' he remarked, then, sliding his hands up the back of her neck, bent his head and kissed her.

Her response was gratifying, and neither of them heard the footsteps outside until the door burst open, and Sir Mark rushed in, his face mottled with rage. Behind him, in the corridor, the earl could see Simon Revell and two other young men, all watching with great interest.

'Shut that damned door!' he said sharply.

Sir Mark ignored him. He was in such fury that it was doubtful if he even heard, and he got his words out only with difficulty.

'How dare you!'

With an exclamation, the earl pushed past Sir Mark and slammed the door in the faces of the fascinated group.

'For God's sake keep your voice down!'

'I won't!'

'Well, you might do so out of regard for Miss Harford,' the earl said with asperity. 'And you can stop enacting me a drama. You are neither betrothed to Miss Harford, nor in any sort her guardian, and I should like to know by what right you came bursting in here!'

'I saw you leading Miss Harford out of the ballroom, and I followed to protect her!'

The earl's lips twitched slightly at the picture of maidenly reserve Sir Mark's words conjured up, and he glanced back at Catherine. She was clutching the shelf, her expression a mingling of horror and enjoyment.

Sir Mark turned to her. 'Miss Harford, come back to

the ballroom with me.' As she hesitated, he said urgently, 'You don't know who this man really is! You have been dazzled by his manners and his position. I do not blame you, but you must know the truth. He is the Black Gentleman! Nothing more than a common highwayman!'

Catherine gasped, and he surged forward, as though to take her hand. 'Aye, I know you must think me mad, but I have seen the proof of it. He is a common highwayman!'

'Don't be a fool,' the earl said, 'or, if you must, don't embroil me in it.'

Sir Mark swung round again. 'You can't cover up with me. I know the truth. You can meet me for it if you wish!'

'I'm more likely to knock you down for it!' He gave an exclamation of impatience as Sir Mark raised his fists. 'Oh, for God's sake. Do you think I am going to engage in a brawl in front of Miss Harford? And keep your voice down or we'll have every gossip-monger in the place coming in on a private quarrel.'

'I've kept silent before when I should have spoken out, but not any more. I'll have you discredited in every house in London before I'm through!'

'And you'll make yourself look the biggest fool in London while you're trying to do it,' the earl returned. 'My credit isn't yet so low that it can't stand up to such a laughable accusation.' He turned to Catherine, still shrinking against the mantelpiece. 'Miss Harford, I'll take you back.'

Sir Mark thrust himself between them. '*I* will take Miss Harford back,' he said savagely. He held out his arm, and the earl stood silent while she looked from one to the other. He knew she was wondering if he would declare himself, and, plainly, if she turned Sir Mark down now, she had lost him forever. He watched as she weighed Sir Mark's definite proposal against his own possible intentions, together with the startling accusation she had just heard. Whilst she could not credit it, something about the complete conviction with which it was made left its mark. She took an uncertain step towards him, then turned and rested her hand on Sir Mark's sleeve. He threw back a look of triumph, and they went out together.

The earl sat down and grinned wryly. As a man of honour, he should really have asked her to marry him. After the speculation their flirtation had given rise to, to be caught kissing the girl in an ante-room was bound to be somewhat damaging to her reputation. Sir Mark he discounted, but Simon Revell and the other two in the corridor were a different matter. He had not, he reflected, acted as a gentleman. On the point of making an offer, he had held back from the certainty that her affections were not in any way engaged. Mercenary considerations would always rule Miss Harford. It was a slight blow to his vanity to be proved right, but he consoled himself with the thought that Sir Mark's annual income would be a sore temptation to any girl.

He considered the threat to expose him, then dismissed it. Now that Catherine had made plain her preference, Sir Mark was not likely to pursue it. Slightly more serious was the presence of Simon Revell and his friends. It depended largely on how much they had overheard, but with the level of Sir Mark's voice it was unlikely that much had been missed. They would be bound to remark on the curious fact that he had evaded a duel with Finchley, when any normal man faced with such an insult would be roaring for his seconds, but his code of morals, though flexible, made him reluctant to put a bullet through Sir Mark for stating the truth.

He stood up and stretched lazily. Definitely, he had been more at home as an agent in enemy France; purely social life could become tedious. He wondered whether to go back to his estates, but his stewards' reports showed that everything was functioning smoothly. He could, of course, stay on with the *ton,* and move to Brighton at the end of the season. Still musing, he stepped into the corridor and walked slowly back to the ballroom. Just inside the doorway, he came upon Lady Constance chatting animatedly with a friend, and remembered that Leonora was riding her grey before breakfast in the morning.

5

5

Leonora surveyed the sky disgustedly. After a week of reasonable weather it had come on to rain, and trailing black clouds were chasing each other above the chimney-pots.

She had wondered whether to take her hack out or not. Of a certainty her velvet riding habit would be ruined if she did. She reached for it doubtfully, and her hand brushed against the one she had brought from Revell House. It was hardly the height of fashion, but it was respectable, and it would take no harm from the wet.

Having made up her mind, she called her abigail who, clearly supposing her to have taken leave of her senses, pointed out the channels of water running down the window-pane.

'I know,' Leonora said briskly. 'But I shan't melt. Where did I put my whip?' She hunted in the bottom of her wardrobe and came out with it, triumphant. 'There we are. That's everything.'

'You'll be drenched,' the maid said. 'It's been pouring since seven this morning.'

As though to contradict her, a pale streak of sunlight broke through and made watery patterns in the raindrops on the window.

'An omen for you,' Leonora said, and went down to wait in the front drawing room. When the grey appeared he was sidling and snorting, as usual, at dangerous things like puddles and pigeons.

'He's in a rare twitter this morning,' the groom informed her, throwing her up into the saddle. Leonora smiled, and sniffed the air appreciatively. The pavements had a wet, earthy smell, and the trees in the distance showed the vivid green of spring. She decided it was a delightful day for a ride, and sent the grey at a swinging trot through the almost empty streets.

Just inside the park gates, she saw a solitary figure walking his horse up and down, and checked for a moment, but Lord Everard had already remarked her, and was turning the black to meet her.

'I've been waiting here for half an hour,' he said plaintively. 'I didn't know what time before breakfast was.'

Leonora reined in and eyed him defensively. 'I'll tell you now, if you're going to be disagreeable again, you can go away.'

'Ah, you mean last night. Now I flatter myself that I did you the world of good.'

'Whatever can you mean!'

'You were sitting there lost in gloom, and I know nothing sets you up like a good quarrel. Now confess it. By the time I left you, you were in fine battling form.'

Leonora grinned. 'You really are the most abominable man, and appallingly rude.'

'I know,' the earl said sympathetically. 'Other men murmur pretty compliments into your ear and encourage you to tread them underfoot. And while we are on the subject, madam, let me inform you that I am accustomed to meeting with more respect than I generally receive from you!'

Leonora chuckled. 'Do you wish me to toady to you? I could do so, of course. I've seen you surrounded by your bevy of flatterers.'

'And you dare to call me abominable! Let's give the horses to your groom and go and sit on that seat.'

'I will not! It's bound to be soaking wet!'

'You've been sitting on a wet saddle for the past half-hour.'

'I know, but I've warmed that,' Leonora pointed out with simple reason.

'One of the things I love about you,' the earl said fondly, 'is your utter want of delicacy. When will you marry me?'

Leonora's hands froze on the reins, and the grey snatched at the bit indignantly. In a peculiar, disembodied way, the earl's words seemed to float round and repeat themselves in her head. Her throat had tightened painfully, but she turned her wide, amber eyes up to him, and said, 'I think you must be joking.'

'Don't be hen-witted,' he said tartly. 'I've just made you a serious proposal of marriage.'

'But you don't even know me!'

'I know you very well. You're reasonably good-looking, though no beauty, and when you're not behaving like a hoyden you have a certain elegance. You're quick-witted, and sharp-tongued, and if someone doesn't take you in hand, you'll be a veritable shrew by the time you're thirty. How old are you, by the way?'

'Nearly one and twenty,' Leonora said, in a small voice.

'Then I should snatch me up,' he advised her kindly. 'You're not likely to receive a better offer at your age. Unless, of course, you favour the little man who floods you with flowers. And there you're at another disadvantage. You must be five foot nine in your shoes.'

'I can't think why you wish to marry me at all,' Leonora said, beginning to be indignant.

'Nor can I,' he confessed with a sigh. 'But then I'm thirty-one, and rapidly approaching the stage where I need someone to warm my slippers for me.'

Leonora giggled, and he eyed her consideringly. 'There is one point I feel I should mention. We cannot overlook the possibility that Finchley may cause a little trouble concerning my reprehensible past. If it is bruited abroad that I was once engaged in highway robbery, I quite understand that you might not wish for such a close association.'

'Then Finchley does know!'

'He can't have any proof, but I confess I should like to know how he did recognise me. Which was why I was questioning you the other day.'

'I saw the white streak in your hair,' Leonora said simply. 'There couldn't possibly be two such large men with the same characteristic.'

'Then we can dismiss him. He was on the other side of the coach where he couldn't see.' He measured her height in the saddle against his own. 'We should make an impressive couple, you and I.'

'I haven't yet said I *will* marry you!'

'Ah, but you will.' His eyes gleamed maliciously. 'I shouldn't have asked you without preparing the ground if I hadn't felt that my feelings were reciprocated. You used to watch me round the ballroom, you know.'

Leonora blushed vividly. 'I did not!'

'But you did!'

'Then I hold it to be very ungentlemanly in you to mention it now. You seem determined to cause me embarrassment every time we meet.'

'You grant me such wonderful opportunities.' There was a warmness in his teasing glance, and Leonora felt a glow of happiness that not even the raindrops trickling down her neck could mar. But the earl, after studying the sky, said he thought they would be well advised to make for home before it became wetter still. With one accord they turned and thudded down the track, her groom at a discreet distance behind, but before they were halfway to the gates a flurry of wind and rain caught them, and plastered her hair down on her face. She laughed, and pushed back the draggled ostrich feather that nodded wetly in front of her nose.

'Oh dear, do let's hurry.'

They raced through the streets, clouds of steam rising from their horses' shoulders, and reined in in front of the house. 'And this time,' the earl said firmly, 'you can wait decorously to be handed down.' He lifted her from the saddle and set her on her feet. 'The groom can take my horse round with yours, and I'll come in and see your father.'

'No,' Leonora said impulsively. 'Not yet.'

He raised his brows.

'Let Paul and Maria make their announcement first. He's waiting to hear from his parents before they make it public.'

'You don't want to rob Maria of her hour of triumph? Very well.'

Leonora said defensively, 'It wouldn't be kind.'

'I'm not arguing,' the earl said mildly. 'Now go in before you take cold.' He raised her hand to his lips. 'I'll call on you tomorrow.'

Bemused, she trailed up the stairs to her room, the skirts of her habit slopping against the banisters. It was the first time she had been submitted to the full force of Lord Everard's charm, and she felt faintly battered. Enduring her maid's reproaches in silence, as she was stripped of her sodden clothes, she tried to overcome her sense of disbelief.

It was well known that he could almost take his pick of all the aristocratic, wealthy beauties in London; they positively flung themselves at his head on every opportunity. And he considered her nothing beyond the ordinary in looks. She was guiltily aware that her only genuine accomplishment was her performance on the pianoforte, and for all she knew, he might not even be musical.

Thinking back over the few times they had met, she was very certain that at Almack's he must have found her insipid. The shock of finding the Black Gentleman, Mark Finchley and herself together had made her temporarily lose her wits. Neither could it be said that she had dazzled him with her sparkling conversation on their first ride.

Without being in any way loud or forceful, the earl had a strong personality. Before he entered her sphere she had thought love at first sight was an emotion dreamed up by silly schoolgirls, but even hidden under a mask his charm of manner had come through, and after one dance at Almack's she admitted she was lost.

Her maid was still fussing round her, predicting an inflammation of the lungs, and she sat patiently, waiting for

her to finish. It was when she was winding her damp ringlets round her fingers to put them back into curl that it occurred to her that the earl did not yet know of their scandalous venture into trade, and she resolved to confess it on
the morrow. Mr. Rochford had been slightly taken aback
when it was disclosed to him, but had large-mindedly
taken their own view that as long as his parents didn't get
to hear of it, it was not of great moment.

She realised that she had not yet breakfasted, and, still
immersed in her reverie, floated down to the parlour
where Simon was consuming cold ham behind a sporting
paper. Since he was widely known for being more than or-
dinarily unobservant, his sister's glowing looks did not impress him. Kindly removing his paper from the coffee-pot,
he volunteered the information that it was fresh, and
pushed the toast towards her.

'Devil of a kick-up at Netherby's last night,' he said. 'I
didn't see you before you left.'

'What about?' Leonora surveyed the toast, and decided
that she was too elated for such mundane matters as food.
She contented herself with pouring out a cup of coffee,
and looked enquiringly across at him.

'Lord, you should have heard it! Everard had got that
copper-head in one of the rooms off the main corridor,
and Mark Finchley got wind of it. You know how it's been
between him and Everard for weeks. You could hear
Finchley roaring like a bull all down the passage.' He
waved a forkful of ham in the air, and Leonora watched
him with painful intensity.

'What happened?'

'Well, we didn't have to listen. You could hear him
through the door, clear as a bell. Mind you,' he added, 'I

can't say we walked away either. There was Everard asking by what right he comes bursting in, and Finchley bawling that he'd get him discredited in all the clubs. Some story about Everard being a highwayman! Everard! I ask you! Funny thing is, you'd have expected Everard to call him out, wouldn't you? But he took it as calm as you please. Then the Harford comes out on Finchley's arm and they go off to the ballroom together. So it looks,' he concluded, 'as though she's settled for Finchley's money after all.'

Leonora whitened slowly. She had read in novels where the blood drained away from the face of the heroine who was about to swoon, but she had never imagined it to be this peculiar prickling of the face and neck. She stared through the window, where a sparrow was frantically gathering up pieces of straw for a nest, but it did not register in her mind. She felt strangely detached, and when she spoke it was as though she was listening to the voice of another person.

'What about Lord Everard being a highwayman?'

'I've told you.' Simon had once more propped his paper against the coffee-pot, and she was thankful her face was hidden from view. 'Finchley said he'd recognised him as the Black Gentleman, or some such thing. We all know Everard's been cutting him out with the red-head, but myself, I think that's coming it a bit too strong. Shouldn't have thought the beauty was worth scrapping over. *I've* never had anything to do with her, but looks ain't everything, and Angus says she's a regular cat with anyone who doesn't measure up to her social standard. Very high and mighty.'

His head ducked lower behind the paper, and he uttered

an exclamation. 'Good God, the Red Heron is running to-morrow!'

Leonora swallowed. 'What if someone else thought they recognised Lord Everard as well?'

'Might be different then, I suppose, but, I mean, is it likely? Everard!' He rose to his feet and patted her shoulder as he went by. 'I'm off to put a bet on this horse. If Angus calls, tell him to wait.'

'You'd better tell Collins,' Leonora said mechanically. 'I may be going out.'

She heard Simon whistling cheerfully as he went to collect his coat, and waited until the front door had slammed behind him before she rose to leave the breakfast parlour. From the hall she could see Lady Constance issuing her orders for the day, and quietly slid past the half-open door. She had a desperate desire to get to her own room without meeting anyone; to lock her door against menus and shopping expeditions and Maria's wedding plans.

Once there, she sank on the bed and waited for the tears she had been fighting back, but now they wouldn't flow. Her face in the dressing-table mirror looked the same as always. She had expected to see some outward mark of what she had just undergone.

So Lord Everard didn't love her! He had only asked her to marry him when Catherine Harford had rejected him and Finchley had threatened to make his knowledge widespread! She remembered the earl's words the first time they had ridden in the park. 'I thought it might not successfully silence you.' Faced with the threat of scandal, or much worse, he had decided he might just as well as eliminate the second danger by marrying Leonora Revell.

Poor Leonora! She stared at her reflection scornfully.

He had been so certain of her! So sure that he had only to raise a finger and she would run to him! Her cheeks flamed when she thought how obvious she must have made herself; how other people must have watched her making a fool of herself and laughed behind her back. She had allowed her common sense to be overborne by the charm of a man of whom she knew nothing. She had even known him to be a highwayman and had not troubled to question his motives or the ethics of it.

What an utter fool she had been! Anyone who was not besotted must have seen through him immediately. A man did not pursue one girl until the whole town was waiting with bated breath for the news of their betrothal, and then, overnight, drop her and propose marriage to a female with whom he was barely acquainted. And only a female lost to all sense of reason would accept him if he did!

He had not even asked her parents' permission to pay his addresses. Not that they would refuse, Leonora thought cynically. Well, at least she had found out in time, and providentially, they had not become officially engaged.

Tears filled her eyes for the first time, and for a moment she wished she had not discovered the truth; she could have been wedded to him in happy ignorance; then her pride reasserted itself. To be married to a man who only pretended love? Her mind went back over the morning. He had never once actually said he loved her; perhaps there were depths to which he would not sink.

She wondered what to say when he came tomorrow, and was seized with a malevolent desire to make him suffer. If he was so afraid of what she might disclose, then he should be made to suffer the more. He could spend his days in suspense, wondering when the blow would fall! Her shoulders, which had squared in a militant manner, drooped again. For one thing, she could not imagine the earl sulking in fear, and for another she was too stupid, too spiritless, too lacking in the desire for a little honest, red-blooded revenge, to wish him the least harm.

She sniffed dolefully, and poured some water into a bowl to bathe her eyes. She had been sitting here half the morning, and Lady Constance would be coming up if she didn't put in an appearance soon. She was thankful once more that she had prevented the earl from speaking to her father. Since they didn't know the dark secret of the Black Gentleman, it would be utterly impossible to give any reasonable explanation for her behaviour, and they would be bound to think she had run mad if she accepted him before breakfast and turned him down at noon. At least she had been spared that.

The day dragged on interminably, and she excused herself from their evening engagement on the grounds of a headache. It was not at all the sort of entertainment where she would expect to find the earl, but the bare possibility of meeting him was enough to set her knees trembling.

Lady Constance, after fussing round her with concern, was at last persuaded to leave without her. She was so seldom unwell that Lady Constance was at first convinced that she must be sickening for some dread disease, and the abigail did not improve matters by triumphantly announcing that she had known Miss would not escape unscathed from her wetting that morning.

Between them Leonora was almost brought to screaming-pitch, but by promising to get between the sheets immediately they were gone, and to drink a measure of Godfrey's Cordial after her hot milk, she induced them to leave her. Her maid's tendency to linger and proffer advice, she overcame by the simple expediency of drawing the bed-curtains firmly around her, and was then left alone with her misery.

She awoke next morning unrested, and with a feeling of panic as she remembered the earl was due to call on her. During the long hours of the night she had decided to write to him, condemning herself for a coward as she did so. Dressing hastily, she went down to inform the butler that she had the migraine and was not at home to anyone who might call, then went back to pen her difficult letter to Lord Everard.

Several times, as lying there in the dark she pondered her problem, she had almost made up her mind to ignore Simon's unhappy revelation. After all, she would be married to him, and in her mama's day it had not been thought necessary to be in love with one's future partner. In fact, the whole idea of falling in love was considered to be a little vulgar, and many couples who were barely acquainted on the day of the wedding had managed to live reasonably happy lives. She had a strong suspicion, however, that such instances were only where each partner was equally indifferent to the other, and she was far from indifferent to Lord Everard.

While no one actually went so far as to term him a rake, he was certainly markedly partial to feminine company, and not only those of his own degree. Once, when she and Maria had been out walking with Mr. Rochford, she had seen him driving his phaeton with an elegant young

woman up beside him. Not recalling her face, she had
turned to ask Mr. Rochford who she might be, and was
met by the glazed expression that overtook him in moments of acute embarrassment. No, she could never be
happy under such circumstances. For an example she need
look no further than Aunt Margaret. Whilst there was no
pretense of love between them, her husband's blatant infi-
delities had caused her severe humiliation over the years.
How much worse, then, must it be in her own case!

She bent over her paper and tried to compose a digni-
fied message. Her first impulse had been to tell him in
scathing terms exactly what she thought of his insulting
proposal, but to do so must inevitably preclude their meeting in future without awkwardness, and it would not be
fair to Maria and Mr. Rochford to be forever battling with
him.

Neither did she feel that under his searching gaze she
could speak the words she was so rapidly writing down.
Not for a moment would he believe her polite excuses that
she felt they would not suit, but if she only avoided meeting him for a while, the worst of the unpleasantness would
be over.

As she signed it, it occurred to her that he had never
once called her by her name, and a slow tear rolled down
her cheek. Disgusted with herself, she mopped it up with
the sleeve of her gown, and took the letter down for Collins to deliver by hand. Aware that Collins had read the
direction and was regarding her doubtfully, she fled to the
safety of her room again, absurdly apprehensive that the
earl might ring the bell while she was in the hallway,

though it was still too early for him to call. She then informed her maid that she was going to try to sleep, and stationed herself behind the curtains to watch for him.

When he did appear, she would have snatched her letter back if she could.

The emotions she had experienced when Simon made his shattering disclosure washed over her again, and she was forced to tell herself not to be a fool—falling for a man only because of his outward appearance and charm. 'As well buy a horse only for its looks,' she told herself. 'A handsome face could conceal a black heart!' It struck her that she was even beginning to think in melodramatic terms, and for the first time in twenty-four hours a choking giggle escaped her. But then she heard the front door closing again, and his footsteps as he descended to the street. He stood for a moment frowning up at the front of the house, then, with a shrug, turned away.

Pensively, he walked home again, wondering what the devil Leonora was about. While it was possible she really did have the migraine, the bald statement from the butler, without any message to soften it, struck him as a calculated evasion. And why, after yesterday, should she wish to avoid him?

The question was resolved when he reached home. Tossing down his hat and gloves on the hall table, he picked up the assortment of correspondence and carried it into the drawing room. It was mostly bills and invitations, but an idea that Leonora may have written caused him to go through until he found her letter. He read the formal phrases with astonishment, and, slipping the letter into his pocket, slammed out of the house again.

Covering the distance back to Leonora's in half the time

it had taken him on the previous journey, he rang a peal on the doorbell. It was answered by the totally impassive butler, but, by great good fortune, he saw Lady Constance crossing from the front room. He bowed, and she came twittering towards him.

'I had hoped to find Miss Revell at home, ma'am,' he informed her.

Lady Constance beamed on him. 'Poor Leonora—she is laid upon her bed with the migraine, but come in and I will see if she is better.'

She ushered him in, and wishing to be personally assured of her daughter's state of health, flitted up to her room.

Leonora heard her with a sinking feeling, as she realised the earl must have read her letter. She cursed the fact that when she had issued her orders to the butler she had forgotten to lay a similar command upon her mother.

'I don't feel well enough,' she protested.

'Do come down,' Lady Constance coaxed. 'It's a lovely day, and if he should want you to drive out with him, I'm sure it would do you good. Though now I come to think,' she added, 'I do believe he was walking. Still, never mind.'

Leonora wilted. It seemed her strategy had gone awry, but since he was actually here, there was no point in putting off the evil hour. He could hardly become excessively violent in her parents' house. She slipped off the bed and ran a comb through her hair, before following her mother out with trembling knees. Any faint hopes she nourished that her mama's sense of propriety would forbid her leaving them alone together were dashed when she got down. The earl's expression was schooled to one of unruffled calm, but as soon as Lady Constance was out of earshot, he frowned across at her, and she found her knees shaking afresh.

'I should like a few words with you in private!'

Smitten dumb, Leonora backed into the drawing room, and waited hopelessly for him to continue. He took the letter from his pocket and laid it on the table. Unable to raise her eyes to his face, she stared at it, and wished her brain would begin to function again.

'Why?'

The single word roused her from immobility, and she found he was regarding her steadily.

'I put it all in my letter,' she faltered. 'I . . .'

'Rubbish,' he interrupted. 'A lot of platitudes and polite evasions. This wasn't in your mind yesterday morning. Don't you think I am entitled to a true explanation?' His voice took on a gentle note. 'Come, Leonora. Surely it is not anything we cannot talk out?'

She gulped. If she had not known of his perfidy, she must have thought there was sincerity in his every word. But it all fitted together too well; his words in the park about silencing her; his break-up with Catherine Harford, and Sir Mark's threat; Simon's words of yesterday. What had he said? It would be different if more than one person told the same tale. And what better person than herself! Backed by her corroboration Mark Finchley's evidence must be damning, for she had no motive for bringing about his downfall.

'I have told you, I put it in my letter,' she repeated.

His voice hardening, he said deliberately, 'I thought you had more courage!'

The edge of scorn in his voice stung her. Why should she stand here apologising for her actions, when all the fault could be laid at his own door?

'No, it isn't the true reason,' she flared, 'but since we must meet frequently, I thought this the best way. Mr. Rochford is your closest friend, and as he is to marry my sister, it would obviously cause a great deal of awkwardness if we cannot be in the same room together!'

'And what have you discovered since yesterday that you cannot endure to be in the same room with me?' There was a hard frown in his eyes, and she felt as many a luckless foot soldier had done in the recent war when they had incurred the censure of Captain Matheson. 'Come, Leonora, I don't pretend to have led a blameless life, but I cannot recall anything you do not already know, sufficient to give rise to this!'

She gasped with indignation, and he said, 'For God's sake let us have a little honesty!'

'You cannot recall anything . . . ! I suppose you have forgotten the incident at Lady Netherby's ball!'

'And who regaled you with that little tale?'

'If you must know, it was Simon, but when he told me he didn't know I was in any way concerned with it!'

'It's a pity he couldn't find a more desirable subject for his sister's delectation,' the earl said sardonically. 'And what precisely did he tell you?'

'That you had taken Catherine Harford . . .' She stopped, as it occurred to her that she did not know whether the earl's intention had been a little light amusement or serious seduction.

Meeting his gaze, she flushed, and he said in a level voice, 'So that is your reason. I see. There doesn't seem to be very much I can say, does there?'

She shook her head dumbly, and he gave her a small bow and walked out.

The outlines of the door blurring through her tears, she ran for her room again, and Mr. Revell, in the act of taking off his coat, looked after her thoughtfully. Entering the drawing room, he saw her letter where the earl had left it on the table. He picked it up and read it, and, more thoughtful than ever, put it carefully away in his pocket.

Lord Everard, slowly retracing his steps, was equally thoughtful. His emotions, as he reviewed what had just taken place, were mixed, and he was puzzled by her behaviour. Where was the fighting, unsquashable Leonora of their previous encounters? If she had roundly taken him to task over the episode with Catherine Harford, he could have understood it. It would have been more in her character, as he knew it. Perhaps she had been right when she protested that he did not know her well enough for marriage, and he had been mistaken in her. Either that or he had mishandled her badly, which he owned could be the case.

It had not been with any intention of proposing that he had waited for her in the rain. Then, it had merely been a desire, unexamined, for her company. After the stilted manners of the débutantes paraded before him, her very candidness appealed to him, and several times he had mulled over her action in warning him of his danger when he held up that dilapidated coach.

When they had met again in London he had been aware of her in a way he had not realised at the time. Not the attraction of Catherine Harford, who, in spite of her beauty, had no genuine appeal for him; manners which were too polished, and remarks made only for their effect, quickly palled on him. Leonora had a deeper appeal.

Her remark about having warmed the saddle had entertained him hugely, and he tried to visualise any other well-brought-up damsel of his acquaintance making a like pronouncement. In that moment, it seemed he had found something that might never come his way again. He knew that he wanted her for his wife.

Perhaps he had mishandled her. Perhaps he should have courted her in the prescribed fashion, and, admittedly, to hear that he had been caught kissing another girl the night before might come as something of a shock. It was also possible that his activities had been exaggerated in the telling, but her attitude still surprised him.

If she did have a prudish streak, he thought, a trifle grimly, she was in for a few more shocks where her brother was concerned. Simon was rapidly becoming one of the leading sparks of the younger set, and unless some sobering influence was brought to bear, he was likely to find himself in more trouble than he imagined.

Like Mr. Rochford, he wondered if he should try to give his thoughts some other direction. Without undue conceit, he felt he could bring more influence to bear on a younger man of Simon's age and disposition than either Mr. Rochford or Mr. Revell, and resolved to take a hand in the matter.

6

Quite by chance, the opportunity to embark on his programme of reformation came sooner than he thought. He and Simon moved in different circles, and for him to deliberately seek the younger man out would be thought odd, but a random visit to Tattersall's, that mecca of the horse world, brought the solution. Engaged in heated argument under the painting of the great Eclipse were Mr. Barnethorpe, a trifle hollow-eyed as usual, Simon, and Lord Angus Delmar.

'And I tell you that three-legged screw hasn't a hope,' Simon was shouting. 'Oriental against the Red Heron! He won't smell him after the first furlong!'

'And I say the Red Heron hasn't been tried over more than seven furlongs before,' Mr. Barnethorpe retorted warmly. 'He goes all out for the first six, then he's done for. No stamina!'

Smiling to himself, the earl strolled over.

'Lay you four to one on the Red Heron, Barney.'

'Everard! Done! What will you put up?'

'I should perhaps tell you,' the earl said apologetically, 'that I have seen the Red Heron in training over ten furlongs, and I have no doubt of his ability to stay the distance.'

'What did I tell you,' Simon said triumphantly. 'Good deep ribs on him, and this new jockey knows how to ride him. You're prejudiced because he's lop-eared, but what I say is, he don't run with his ears!'

'Ears ain't anything to do with it,' Lord Angus said, shaking his head. 'Oriental won over ten furlongs last month, and my money's on him. Lay you a pony,' he added hopefully.

'Done!' Simon said with enthusiasm. He suddenly recalled his company, and caught Lord Everard's eye.

The earl smiled easily. 'You're young Revell, aren't you? Well, stick to your choice.' He turned back to Mr. Barnethorpe. 'I'll lay you a pony, and give you four to one.'

'You're on! Thought you weren't a betting man?'

'You were misinformed,' the earl returned tranquilly, 'but I only gamble for pleasure.'

'So does everybody!'

'Oh no,' the earl said. 'Think of poor Brummell! Now I must confess that the idea of waking up one morning without the means to purchase the comforts of life quite sends a chill down my spine!' He smiled gently, and Mr. Barnethorpe and Lord Angus, both backed by wealthy parents, grinned at him. It was widely known that the earl had been a daring agent in the war; his exploits were still recounted in the clubs, and he had been mentioned in Wellington's despatches. Only Simon, in whom the desire to keep up with his friends was constantly at odds with an acute business sense, suspected that perhaps he had not spoken in jest. Their eyes met for a moment, then the earl turned back to the others.

'I was thinking of setting up a racing stable. Morton has a very pretty mare for sale.'

Simon, in whom horses were a passion, forgot that he had never dared so much as to nod to the earl before, and plunged whole-heartedly into the discussion that followed. With a reckless disregard for his purse, they planned the nucleus of the earl's stable, and argued over the design of the buildings where they would be housed.

'And I'll tell you who to get to ride 'em,' Simon said. 'There's a postboy down at the White Hart. Little fellow with a limp. They stuck him on a devilish screw the only time he ever raced, but he's a natural if ever I saw one. Knows just how to nurse his horse along and get the best out of him.'

The earl thanked him gravely, and Simon stood over him while he made a note of the name. 'Snap him up, or, mark my words, someone else will get him first!' It occurred to him that giving advice to one of the leading men of the sporting world might be considered presumptuous, but Lord Everard seemed very relaxed and informal, and showed no sign of taking offense.

'Are you going to watch the race this afternoon?'

Simon shook his head. 'I didn't know the horse was running until this morning, and Barney and Angus have got something else planned.'

'There is room in my curricle if you want to come with me,' the earl offered casually.

Hardly able to believe his ears, Simon said, 'I should rather think I would!' He added respectfully, 'Sir.'

'Be at my house in an hour's time.' He nodded to Simon, and punched Mr. Barnethorpe on the shoulder. 'I'll collect my money off you tomorrow!'

Mr. Barnethorpe uttered a derisive roar, and, grinning broadly, the earl walked out.

Hurrying home to change into garments more suitable to his company, Simon dwelled with anticipation on the afternoon ahead. Besides the attraction of the magnificent pair of blacks which drew the curricle, he was still young enough to be flattered by an invitation from a man of Lord Everard's standing. His mind returned briefly to the incident at the ball, and he was faintly embarrassed at being caught listening outside doors like a schoolboy. It was no business of his how Everard conducted his *affaires,* and he was relieved to find the earl apparently attached no importance to his eavesdropping.

Finding all the family assembled at home, he was unable to resist the temptation to mention in passing that he was accompanying Lord Everard to the races. His sisters, he felt, were getting above themselves since they had begun mixing freely with the *ton.*

Leonora, a little dark under the eyes, had abandoned her migraine. She found it was less exhausting to try to appear normal in company than to have Lady Constance forever trekking up to her room to check on her state of health. To give her hands something to do, she was engaged in trimming a hat, an occupation which caused her mother further alarm, since she was notoriously poor at all forms of stitchery.

When Simon had gone, she raised her eyes from her uninspiring task, and commented acidly that she hoped Lord Everard would not lead Simon into expensive company.

'No reason to think he will,' Mr. Revell said. 'He's always seemed a sensible sort of man, and he's bound to know Simon can't afford the sort of pastimes he does himself. Good of him to take him along.'

Lost for a reply, Leonora bent over her stitching again. It seemed she could never go anywhere without hearing the earl's praises sung: now her father and Simon had joined the band of his admirers.

Certainly Mr. Revell was happy to find his heir in such unexceptional company. Far too wise a parent to waste his breath on remonstrances which would go unheeded, he was nevertheless worried. The worst that could be said of Lord Everard was that he was a notorious flirt. His pursuits definitely did not include riotous expeditions in doubtful company into Spitalfields and Seven Dials. The Watch and Bow Street Runners, by tacit consent, seldom ventured into these districts, and the young bloods had little protection but their fists if they fell foul of the thieves and murderers abounding in the noisome alleys. Neither was the earl a member of the fraternity who risked huge sums of money every night in the tail end of London's gambling frenzy. If an afternoon at the races under his aegis would give Simon's thoughts another turn, Mr. Revell was disposed to be grateful.

He regarded Leonora pensively. The smudges under her eyes were marked, and she wore a dispirited air. Remembering the contents of her letter, it seemed that young love had gone awry, but the earl struck him as a man well able to manage his own affairs; he could not see that interference on the part of a mere parent would serve any useful purpose.

Interrupting his thoughts, the door banged noisily behind his departing son. Simon, out of deference to his company, had abandoned the handkerchief he commonly wore knotted around his neck and had attempted an Osbaldiston Tie with his moderate neckcloth. The result was not entirely happy, and he was torn between making another attempt, and possibly being late, or going as he was and arriving punctually. He decided on punctuality, for which he was thankful, when the earl with a swing of his many-caped driving coat, came down to join him before he had mounted the first step.

As soon as they swung up into the curricle, the famous blacks were anxious to be off, fretting and cantering on the spot. Simon, himself no mean whip, watched how the earl held them with his long, flexible fingers, firm yet light, and felt a stab of envy.

'They're a damned fine pair!' he said.

'Yes.' The earl gently eased off the reins, and they surged forward. 'I'm trying to match them for a team, but either they won't go together or one of them shows brown by the others. It's amazing how rarely you find a true black. You can try them as soon as we're clear of the traffic.'

Almost overcome, Simon thanked him. 'You don't even know that I'm fit to drive them!'

'I did check,' the earl admitted. 'My head groom has seen you with a pair, and appears to think you capable.'

'My father used to keep some good cattle. Hunters and hacks as well. Bred them himself for years, though there wasn't much sport around us.'

'Your sister is an intrepid horsewoman,' the earl commented, guiding the blacks adroitly round a delivery wagon. 'That grey of hers is no novice's ride.'

'Leonora! Oh she'll get on anything; always been a

devil to go! Then there's Maria, won't even sit on anything with a spark of life.'

'They appear dissimilar in many respects,' the earl prodded gently.

'They are. Maria ain't got a word to say for herself half the time. Quite a beauty, though, and not a scrap of harm in her.'

'And Leonora . . . ?' the earl prompted, fostering this brotherly candour. Dissatisfaction lurked at the back of his mind. Admitted, their acquaintance was not of long duration, but the Leonora who could accept his double identity without a blink was oddly at variance with the Leonora who had rejected his suit. 'She has always seemed a very . . . spirited young woman.'

'She is. Makes my mother nervous taking her about. Inclined to take a bit of a dig at the old tabbies when she forgets herself. She'll never get married off if she don't watch her tongue!'

Cherishing the picture these words conjured up, the earl said, 'She doesn't appear to lack for suitors.'

'No,' Simon admitted. 'She could have had Finchley at one time, and apparently he's a regular catch. She suddenly went off him though. Threw my mother into the devil of a pucker when it happened.'

This was news to the earl, and he was interested. 'When was this?'

'Oh, way back last year.' Simon paused to admire the way the earl manoeuvered a tricky portion of the road. 'Finchley was haunting the place, and he'd practically come to the point.'

'And then?'

'Oh, there was some to do. I remember! It was the night

she was held up by a highwayman! She said Finchley sat his horse as though he was stuffed when she was in direst peril. At least, that's what she told my mother.'

The earl shook with silent laughter. 'Was she in direst peril?'

'I don't really see how she could have been from what I heard, but apparently what she meant was that Finchley didn't know that. It gets complicated. I don't see it myself, but you know what females are!'

The earl allowed himself a moment of pure enjoyment. 'What did Lady Constance have to say?'

'Said there was no point in Finchley getting himself shot!'

'A refreshingly practical viewpoint,' the earl commented, with deep appreciation. 'You may take the reins!' He handed them over, and leaned back with folded arms. The Leonora of this morning's unhappy interview was more out of character than ever.

He searched back through his mind for any other cause than the obvious conclusion he had come to, but the precise sequence of events responsible for Leonora's heart-burnings did not manifest themselves. Nevertheless, he became convinced that it was based on a misunderstanding, and congratulated himself on his resolve to take the erring brother in hand. His motives had been excellent, and they had served a double purpose. The little sidelights on his beloved were more illuminating.

The mood engendered by Leonora's reception of him that morning now completely dispersed, he settled back to watch Simon. They had come up with an enormous stage wagon, drawn by eight heavy horses, all wearing bells to warn of their approach. It took up a major portion of the road, and Lord Everard's pair took instant and grave exception to its presence. Several times Simon had them edged up to overtake when the driver's whip would come snaking out, or a deeper rut in the road would set the rumbler bells jangling louder than ever.

'Damnation!' Simon said. If anything, the road narrowed further ahead.

The earl held out his hand. 'Give them back to me!'

He turned and grinned at the groom on the back. 'Hang on, Jefferson! I'm not promising not to put us in the ditch, but I shall use my utmost endeavour to avoid it!' He held his pair back until he could see clearly for some distance beyond the wagon. 'Here we go!'

With a flick of his whip, he sent them into a gallop, and braced himself to hold them on course. As they neared the wagon, they veered away, and the offside wheel skidded over the grass verge. Simon, his eyes riveted on a milestone half hidden in the grass ahead of them, clutched the side of the curricle and almost offered up a prayer, but the earl, sending his whip along the outside, held them on the road, and they galloped by.

The passengers in the stage wagon sent up a cheer, and Simon let out his breath. In any other man he would have described the action as foolhardy; in the earl it was precision and competence amounting to brilliance.

He was checking their speed now, gradually bringing them down to a trot, and Jefferson loosed his hold upon his hat.

'If I might mention it, my lord, that milestone was a *little* bit close. Whistled by the wheel my side!'

'Are you criticising or commending me, Jefferson?' the earl returned cheerfully. 'Whichever the case, you may save your breath and blow up the toll. It's round the next bend.' He handed the reins to Simon again, and squinted up at the sky. 'I hope the weather holds. I must confess that I am not quite so certain of the Red Heron's chances if the going should turn heavy.'

'I'll still back him against Oriental,' Simon asserted. 'Barney and Angus can stick to their choice, and I'll stick to mine.'

'It doesn't always do to follow Barney's lead in everything,' the earl agreed blandly. 'Still, each to his own pursuits, and I am the first to admit that he can be highly entertaining company.'

Simon coloured, and shot him a quick glance, but by this time they had drawn up at the toll-gate, and he was saved the necessity of replying to the earl's pointed speech. He was well aware that he was being subtly lectured, but while, coming from the older generation, he might have resented it, from an illustrious sportsman who had just demonstrated his supreme ability with a difficult pair it had a different effect. The pastimes to which he knew the earl was alluding suddenly seemed more akin to the juvenile escapades of his university days.

Watching for the effect of his words, Lord Everard thought back over his own past, and damned himself wryly for a hypocrite. By way of atonement, he gave Simon some instruction in the finer points of driving, and by the time they reached the racecourse, Simon was calling him Everard, and treating him with a mixture of awe and familiarity he could not have foreseen earlier in the day. The earl insulted him good-humouredly, treating him very much as he would have done a younger brother, and Simon regarded his lightest word as gospel.

Ruefully, Lord Everard realised he had unwittingly taken on a greater responsibility than he intended. He had envisaged his role as that of some light-hearted mentor, offering guidance and advice, not an example for Simon to pattern himself on.

They gave the curricle into Jefferson's charge, and mingled with the crowd, exchanging opinions on form. Simon made his selection and placed his bet for the first race, and they found a good place and stationed themselves by the rails. Lord Everard had the felicity of watching his choice come in a comfortable winner; Simon's, to his disgust, could only achieve eighth out of a field of nine. Grumbling, he went to place his money for the next race, and, to his surprise, the earl, instead of staking his winnings, as he would have done himself, contented himself with his original stake. Nor did he show any signs of frustration when the horse again came in first.

The third race was the one in which the Red Heron was running. He was not impressive in the first five or six furlongs, and Simon could pick out his reddish colour and lop ears with the stragglers at the rear. But as the leaders began to fall back, blown, his long, even stride carried him past them, and he and Oriental swept into the front. Simon jumped up and down on the spot, loudly exhorting his choice to greater effort, and inch by inch the lop ears crept into the lead and past the winning post.

'He's done it!' Simon shouted, clapping the earl on the shoulder. 'Wait until I see Barney and Angus!'

'No need to beat me,' the earl complained. 'I want to see Barney myself. Do you want to stay for the rest?'

Simon thought it a pity to go before the end, so they placed their bets again. Once more the earl hung on to his

winnings and not wishing to appear in the light of a reckless gambler, Simon did likewise.

He was glad of his restraint when the horse lost dismally, and the earl reflected that sometimes virtue brought its
own reward. If he had not been so busy setting an example
of moderation, he would undoubtedly have followed his
normal custom of putting his winnings on the next race
and would have lost the lot. He felt there must be a moral
somewhere.

They located Jefferson and drove back, the earl going
by way of Simon's home to drop him off. Outside the
house, Simon was afflicted with an attack of shyness. Barney or Angus he would have invited to dine with them, but
the earl was a different matter. And though not normally
given to deep thought, it did occur to him that this was a
guest his mother might like notice of. He compromised by
inviting him in for a glass of wine, and rather to his surprise the earl accepted.

From the number of voices coming from the drawing
room it sounded as though the whole family was home,
and Simon excused himself to the earl and went to ask
Lady Constance if it was convenient to ask him to dine.

She assured him that nothing could be better. 'For Mr.
Rochford is here as well. He is to take us to the theatre afterwards.'

Emboldened, Simon went back to the earl. 'All the family's home, I'm afraid,' he ended apologetically. 'But
Paul's staying as well. He's taking my mother and the girls
out.'

Lord Everard demurred on the grounds that he was not
dressed for dinner, but Simon made light of it, so the earl,
smitten with an unworthy desire to see Leonora's face

when she found she was sharing a table with him, graciously accepted.

He crossed to the drawing room in Simon's wake, and for just a moment was able to see her before she was aware of his presence. She was sitting listlessly by the piano, but she looked up as Lady Constance bustled forward to greet him. He watched her expression progress through defiance to utter indignation when she found he was staying to dine.

Quite naturally, Lady Constance placed them next to one another at the table. Under cover of the general conversation she hissed, 'You might at least have spared me this!'

The earl glanced sideways at her, amused. 'Nonsense! I was merely trying to dispel any little awkwardness you might feel after this morning. Dear me, was it only this morning!' He regarded her blandly for a moment. 'May I help you to some chicken?'

'You're insufferable!' Leonora said, stiff with rage.

'A most unjust observation! You said yourself that it would be uncomfortable if we could not meet in company without at least the appearance of civility, so,' he said, helping himself to a portion of chicken, 'I was practising!'

Leonora drew a deep breath, but Lady Constance leaned forward, smiling brightly. 'I hope you had a pleasant afternoon at the races, Lord Everard.'

'Most agreeable, thank you.' He smiled at Mr. Revell. 'Your son has the makings of a very fair whip, sir.'

'He's promising,' Mr. Revell admitted. As Simon flushed with pleasure, he added, 'A little hot-headed and impatient, but those are faults that time will frequently cure.'

'I don't know what you hope to gain by ingratiating yourself with the rest of my family,' Leonora muttered viciously.

'The rest of your family,' the earl said piously, 'accept me at my true worth.'

'They don't know you as I do!'

'And apart from one discreditable interlude, just what do you know that they don't?' the earl said swiftly. For a moment he thought he had goaded her into a true reply, but she recovered herself. 'I refuse to discuss it!'

'Craven,' the earl sighed. 'And you can't possibly insult me properly without your mother hearing you.' She glared at him, and he smiled back. 'That's better. I don't like to see you looking low.'

Leonora blinked at the unexpected kindness in his voice. His sudden switch in manner disconcerted her, and if they had been alone, she felt she might have given way to her inclination and sobbed on his shoulder. She was silent, and in the pause Lady Constance claimed his attention once more.

'If you are not already committed for this evening, Lord Everard, perhaps you would care to join us at the theatre. With three women to escort, I'm sure Paul would welcome your support. Mr. Revell has another engagement, and Simon will never accompany us.'

'I was engaged, but as it happens, it has been cancelled.' He glanced at Leonora, and added innocently: 'This morning!' She shot him a fulminating look, and he continued smoothly: 'I shall be happy to accept your invitation, Lady Constance.'

Continuing his policy of meddling, he turned his attention to her son. 'Doesn't Simon care for the theatre?'

After his pointed address earlier in the day Simon knew that the earl had a very good idea of what his plans for the evening were, and squirmed uncomfortably in his seat.

'Not very much in my line,' he said.

'The truth of the matter,' Mr. Rochford said disapprovingly, 'is that he ain't even been to find out!'

'Really!' Without in any way being impolite, the earl's tone implied faint shock, and Mr. Revell, at the head of the table, regarded him appreciatively.

'We could get him into the box without too much of a squeeze,' Mr. Rochford said, closing the trap. 'Supposed to be a very good play. Broaden his outlook!'

Simon didn't want his outlook broadened, but he knew when he was beaten. He capitulated, and Lord Everard and Mr. Rochford flashed messages of congratulation to each other.

The meal came to a leisurely close, and Lord Everard went home to change, and returned with his own carriage to take the party's increased numbers. He was highly entertained when Lady Constance, bent upon matchmaking, manoeuvered Leonora in with him, Simon making up the third.

Leonora's softened mood by now had disappeared. A coalition between Lord Everard and her mama had the immediate effect of setting up her hackles, and she refused to open her lips until they reached the theatre.

They were settled in the box, preparing to study the other members of the audience, when Mr. Rochford gave the earl a sharp nudge. Following the direction of his agonised gaze, the earl discovered the dowager countess and his ward.

'Got Digby with her,' Mr. Rochford whispered. 'Not at

all the thing! Only been widowed five months! What's more, she's seen us!'

The earl, feeling that this time his duty was inescapable, murmured that she would be seeing him again in the interval and turned back to Leonora. She was severely handicapped by the presence of her mother, and bestowed an unwilling civility. Lady Constance beamed on them. Lord Everard, attentive to her daughter's every comfort, definitely bore the appearance of a suitor, and if such a marriage could be brought about, it would exceed her highest hopes.

In the first interval the earl, reluctantly but swiftly, made his way to the countess's box, and surprised her, emerging equally swiftly, in an effort to avoid him.

He bowed. 'Madam! Ah, and my ward! I would have called on you, but when you left so suddenly you failed to furnish me with your address.' He smiled at the visibly quaking Sarah. 'I fear I've been a poor guardian. Though your circumstances forbid balls and parties, there are quieter entertainments I could have introduced you to.'

He paused, wondering how to detach her from her mother, then saw Mr. Rochford with Maria and Simon. He made them known to one another, and charged Mr. Rochford with keeping her out of the way. They moved off down the corridor, and the earl and his cousin by marriage eyed one another.

'Before you say anything,' the countess began, 'let me make it plain that my actions are no concern of yours!'

'None at all,' the earl agreed amiably, 'except where they concern your daughter. And when you bring her to a public play when she is in deep mourning, and, what is more, in the company of Digby, you are damaging her reputation to the extent where I must be involved. For goodness' sake, Caroline, haven't you any relatives you could put the girl with?'

'Only you!' she said, with satisfaction.

The earl grinned reluctantly. 'A hit! Give me your direction before the others come back, and I'll call on you tomorrow. Something has got to be sorted out or she'll be ruined! I suppose she's too old to be sent back to school?'

'Use your wits, Louis,' the countess said scornfully. 'She's nearly eighteen!' Her eyes went past the earl. 'Here come the others. Pretty little thing with Paul Rochford, but empty-headed. I prefer the older girl.'

'Caroline, if it wasn't for your predilection for creating scandals, I could like you very well,' the earl told her. 'Now, just to please me, will you take the girl home, and we'll see what can be settled in the morning.'

She nodded, and he escorted them down, and waited while their carriage was sent for. Mr. Rochford was lying in wait for him when he got back.

'Not sure you did the best thing there, dear boy.'

'Why not? I got her to go home, which was more than I had bargained for.'

'No, no, not that,' Mr. Rochford corrected. 'Did very well there. No, I meant landing the girl with us like that.'

The earl waited patiently for him to come to the point.

'It's young Revell. Smitten!' he said succinctly.

'I thought his tastes ran to something more exotic!'

'So did I! Seen him with some very dashing pieces, but I heard him arranging to call on her, and he's sitting there in the box with his head in the clouds.'

'Oh well,' the earl said philosophically. 'If he takes up with her, Leonora will really have something to complain about.'

The rest of the evening was not an unqualified success. During his absence Leonora, with space for a little quiet reflection, had decided to put a stop, once and for all, to both the earl's advances and her mother's hopes. Her manner was so quelling that Lord Everard felt that a lesser man would have given up, and Lady Constance rearranged the seating for their return home, both to shorten her embarrassment and to give her an earlier opportunity of telling her daughter precisely what she thought of her conduct.

'I was never so mortified in my life!' she declared. 'Heaven knows I've had cause to blush for you in the past, Leonora, but your behaviour tonight . . .' She leaned back against the squabs and closed her eyes. 'I think you must be going out of your mind,' she said despairingly. 'I know you'll send me out of mine! One of the most eligible men in town, besides being a friend of Paul's, and being so kind to Simon!'

'If Simon wants to toady to him . . .' Leonora interrupted scornfully.

'I'll give you toadying!' Simon returned wrathfully. 'He's a damned good fellow, and I don't like being put to the blush because my sister can't keep a civil tongue in her head!'

'And a blind man could see he was trying to fix his interest with you,' Lady Constance said. 'When you wouldn't have Sir Mark there was some excuse, for I must admit he wasn't quite what I had hoped for you, but our situation was desperate then. Though if Catherine Harford doesn't despise him . . . still that's neither here nor there. Lord Everard is an entirely different matter. You couldn't find a more pleasant, agreeable man anywhere in England.'

'Lord Everard is not acceptable to me as a suitor,' Leonora said stonily.

Lady Constance flung up her hands. 'I don't know what it is that you want! At Revell House you complained that you were buried in the country, and never met a soul, and now we are come to London and the most personable man pays his addresses to you, and that does not satisfy you either!'

For a moment, Leonora hovered on the brink of informing her that this paragon's courtship was nothing more than a dishonourable attempt to safeguard himself. Probably his kindness to Simon was because he had been a witness to the scene at Lady Netherby's ball, and it was obviously desirable that he should not have the slightest doubt that Sir Mark's accusation was false.

But whatever he had done, she could not be the one to bring about his downfall. She said tiredly, 'I think you are making too much of it, Mama. You've no reason to think he means more than with any of his flirts. I'm sorry,' she added. 'I still have the migraine. It's making me snappish.'

She was glad to get to her room, but when she sat down at the dressing table to remove her ear-rings she saw the bunch of artificial flowers in the mirror frame. She felt that she was probably a very unsatisfactory daughter.

7

Lord Everard, not entirely at his ease in his role of guardian, presented himself on the countess's doorstep on the following morning. It was an elegant house, situated in one of the quieter streets, and even if it was rented, the earl could not see how her finances could support it. She received him in the expensively furnished drawing room, and he let out his breath in exasperation.

'Caroline, don't you care what's going to be said of all this?'

'No,' she returned frankly. 'Precious few come to see it, and those who do can say what they please. After eighteen years I'm free, and I'm not going to sit in the country in my blacks and pretend a grief that everyone knows I can't possibly feel. I'm not such a hypocrite!'

'Don't you think you are presenting Sarah with a slightly doubtful set of standards?' the earl asked mildly.

The countess stared at him. 'Do you know, Louis, I never thought you could turn prudish! Especially since you set the town by the ears with the Harford chit! Lord, Sarah will find out soon enough that the world isn't what her governess has been telling her! Besides, she doesn't know where the money for this comes from. I told her you make us a generous allowance.'

'I was making you a generous allowance,' the earl said plaintively. 'And when you departed so suddenly I instructed my lawyers to trace you so that you might continue to receive it. I admit that the Dower House was not the acme of comfort and elegance, but I made it plain that the arrangement was only temporary. What are you going to do about Digby? Or do I have to call him out?'

'You wouldn't!' the countess said quickly.

'If you won't co-operate, I not only would, but I shall!' He watched her calculating this possibility, and the alarm faded from her face. For him to call Digby out would increase the scandal tenfold, and she realised he would be extremely reluctant to do so.

He sighed. 'Haven't you any friends you could place Sarah with? What about that cousin-companion, Harriet, or whatever her name was? Wouldn't she do?'

'Henrietta! She had hysterics the last time I wrote, and I was only enquiring after her health! No.' She pondered for a moment. 'If you don't like the present arrangement, I think, as her guardian, that you are the proper person to find a suitable alternative!'

And that, the earl acknowledged to himself, was that. He doubted if it would be any use appealing to her instincts as a mother. He was inclined to think that maternal feelings came a poor second to her attachment to Digby. As she pointed out, he was the proper person to make alternative arrangements. He cast round in his mind for any matrons with whom he was well enough acquainted to saddle with his ward, and was unable to think of one who wouldn't suffer a spasm at the mere suggestion.

Accepting defeat gracefully, he went in search of Mr. Rochford and found him at his home.

'Defeated on all points,' he said, lowering himself into a chair. 'Are you engaged with Maria this afternoon or will you be coming to the club?'

'She's out buying wedding finery. What do you mean, defeated on all points? You're talking in riddles lately, dear boy. Still don't know what you meant yesterday about Leonora complaining.'

'The two are connected. Leonora might complain, if through me her brother became involved with my scandalous, portionless ward. I therefore went to see my cousin Caroline, and without precisely laughing in my face, she made it quite plain that if it troubles me, it is up to me to salvage Sarah's reputation.'

'So what are you going to do?'

'I don't know,' the earl admitted. 'But no doubt something will suggest itself. It's quite possible that you read too much in the signs when she and Simon met.'

'If it was me, I shouldn't be worrying about Sarah while Finchley was going round shouting the odds,' Mr. Rochford said frankly. 'I told you you ought to marry Leonora.'

'I asked her to,' the earl said reflectively, 'but she wouldn't!'

'Eh!' Mr. Rochford's eyes popped. 'Never said a word to me! Why won't she marry you?'

'She doesn't think we should suit!' The earl's expression was bland.

'More likely because of the kick up you caused with the copper head!'

'Yes, that's what I thought,' the earl mused. 'But now I'm inclined to think I was wrong. I made my honourable proposal on the morning after the Netherby's ball; and not for the motives you would ascribe to me either,' he added.

'At the time, she wouldn't let me tell her father because she wanted you to make your own announcement first.' He gazed pensively into space. 'Now immediately afterwards, brother Simon, in all innocence apparently, told her about the little incident at the ball.' He transferred his gaze to Mr. Rochford. 'You heard about that, I suppose.'

Mr. Rochford said scornfully, 'The whole town's heard about it!'

The earl nodded. 'Next morning, Leonora wouldn't see me, and sent a note to say she'd thought it over and decided we wouldn't suit. At least that was the gist of it. I managed to see her later, and found Simon had told her about the . . . er . . . incident. I deduced from what she said that this was the basis for her rejection.'

'Thought you'd proposed to her in a fit of pique,' Mr. Rochford said intelligently.

'But do you think,' the earl continued, 'that Leonora is the sort of girl who would be silly enough to believe that, or who would be shocked by my little escapade with the fair Catherine?'

Mr. Rochford thought long and hard, and finally delivered up his verdict. 'No,' he said.

'No more than I!'

'I thought, myself, that she had a *tendre* for you!'

'So did I, or I should have conducted a more formal courtship. So now all I have to do is discover what bee Leonora has in her bonnet. Meanwhile,' the earl continued cheerfully, 'we have, you must admit, a most entertaining situation. Leonora is highly offended with me, and Lady Constance, in happy ignorance, is industriously promoting a match by every means at her disposal.'

'I wondered what was the matter. Created a bit of an atmosphere last night.'

'Yes. I feel we're in for a merry wooing.' The earl smiled tranquilly and placed his fingertips together. 'If Leonora should let fall anything that throws some light on the matter, you might let me know.'

'I'm not getting involved,' Mr. Rochford said firmly. 'Going to be my sister-in-law. Besides, I don't want a dressing down. It ain't that I'm frightened of her, but she's got a sharp tongue. What with the Black Gentleman, and gallivanting over France, then Finchley saying his piece, and Leonora knowing the whole thing, I ain't had a moment's peace of mind in six months. And on top of that I've had a note from my mother to say she's coming to town in a few days.' He regarded the earl gloomily. 'M'sister's expecting her first this month. Thought it might keep her away, but it hasn't.'

The earl's eyes glinted. 'You don't think she might like to take on my ward and make her respectable?'

'If you don't mind my saying so, dear boy, I'd like it better if you kept away from her. Got the impression that she didn't quite take to you when we went to stay.'

'All will be forgiven now that you are about to enter into a respectable alliance.'

A slightly guarded look overspread Mr. Rochford's features. 'Bit inclined to dwell on things, my mother.'

'Oh,' said the earl, pulling himself to an upright position. 'So there's a skeleton in the family cupboard, is there?'

'No, there ain't,' Mr. Rochford said defiantly.

'There is! I knew there was something odd about the

whole business when they arrived in London. The pair
they had in harness when I held her up would have disgraced a hackney! I asked you if there had been an upswing in their fortunes!'

'Nothing to do with you,' Mr. Rochford said, abandon-
ing prevarication as useless.

'That is where you are wrong! I shall marry Leonora
whatever her present sentiments may be!'

'No harm in telling you, I suppose. My mother would
cut up a bit stiff if she knew, and Lady C says it would get
them thrown out of Almack's. A blessing if you ask me.
Devilish place!'

'It's connected with the way they made their money?'
the earl prompted patiently.

'That's right. They gave out it was from coal, but actually the old man bought a mill in Lancashire and went into
manufacturing. Sold up now, of course, and put the money
back into the land, but you can't blame them for not wanting it known. Bound to cause a bit of a stir. Not socially
acceptable!'

The earl shook with laughter. 'I'll bet they made a piece
of work over telling you. Did they think you might cry
off?'

'Seemed a bit worried. Don't see why. It don't bother
me!'

'And it wouldn't bother Leonora either, so her attitude
can't be anything to do with that. I'll see what I can get
out of Simon.'

'What are you up to there?' Mr. Rochford demanded
suspiciously. 'Bear leading ain't in your line.'

'Merely weaning him from his present pastimes—with

the most disinterested of motives!' He rose to his feet and stretched. 'Do we look in at White's? They haven't seen much of you recently.'

Mr. Rochford pronounced himself agreeable, and they stepped down to the street. It was raining, and loftily disregarding Mr. Brummell's maxim that no gentleman would ever be seen in one, they hailed a hackney to take them to the club.

Ever perceptive of atmosphere, Lord Everard detected a slight constraint as he entered the clubroom. He walked across to the bow window, where Lord Alvanley and Sir Henry Mildmay were sitting with their backs to him, and said equably, 'Who's talking about me, William?'

'Ah.' Lord Alvanley moved his chair slightly to make room for them. 'As a matter of fact, we weren't so much discussing you as the deplorable Finchley. He's spreading the most disagreeable rumours, you know.'

'It had reached my ears.'

Lord Alvanley gently swung his quizzing glass on the end of its ribbon. 'What are you going to do about it?'

'Go for trial by my peers,' the earl returned promptly.

'I thought that had all died out years ago,' Sir Henry said plaintively. ' 'Fraid I shouldn't be any use to you anyway. Not a peer.'

'Something should be done about Finchley, all the same,' Lord Alvanley said. 'You'll have to call him out. Fellow's a commoner,' he added dispassionately.

'I hate early rising without good reason,' the earl complained. 'Do I really have to get up at the crack of dawn merely to put a bullet through him?'

'Who's Everard going to put a bullet through?' Mr. Barnethorpe demanded, coming up behind them.

Lord Alvanley and Mr. Rochford eyed him with disapproval, and the earl said, 'You owe me a pony, Barney.'

Mr. Barnethorpe flung up his hands. 'I know! I know! The wretched animal won. Simon was round with the news before I was out of my bed this morning!' He cocked an eyebrow. 'But who is Everard calling out? Or is it a secret?'

'Finchley, unless he minds his manners,' Mr. Rochford said.

'I wondered if I ought to tell you about that,' Mr. Barnethorpe said. 'He's been a bit queer ever since the Beauty got her hooks into him, but he'll really have to be stopped!' He seized the back of a chair enthusiastically. 'I'll be a second!'

The earl grinned. 'No one who has seen you first thing in the morning would ever have you for their second! Besides, I haven't called him out yet. We were discussing the matter academically.'

'Always rely on me in an affair of honour,' Mr. Barnethorpe said, shocked.

'No,' Mr. Rochford said, shaking his head. 'Might get himself up, but he wouldn't be able to tell one end of a duelling pistol from the other. Never can see straight until the day's half gone!'

Mr. Barnethorpe began, ferociously, to defend himself, and with a slight smile the earl set up a fresh topic of conversation with Sir Henry.

To avoid calling Finchley out was going to be something of a problem; his reputation at Manton's was such that no one believed he could miss, and to fire into the air was unthinkable: that was to acknowledge himself guilty. He reflected that few men could have wrestled with the problem of how to avoid winning a duel, and wondered how long he could escape issuing his challenge. His wartime exploits were too well known for his courage to be in doubt, but already his behaviour was considered off. He had caught the faint shade of surprise on Alvanley's face when he changed the subject.

As he and Mr. Rochford left the club, Mr. Rochford said gloomily, 'Wish we hadn't come.'

'It did turn out to be rather the wrong moment.'

'What will you do?'

'If I do have to call him out,' the earl shrugged, 'I shall just have to miss, I suppose.'

'You might just as well fire into the air and have done with it. Can't have a reputation for hitting the wafer every time, then miss something as big as Finchley. Won't wash! I knew this would happen,' he added. 'You go round holding up respectable citizens with a brace of pistols, then drop yourself right in the middle of them and don't expect anyone to notice.'

'What has happened? You've been prophesying death and disaster from the beginning. Now Finchley has done his worst, and, exactly as I foretold, no one chooses to believe him. If it weren't for my nice sense of honour which makes me reluctant to shoot him, we shouldn't be in any difficulty at all.'

'*We* ain't in difficulty,' Mr. Rochford said firmly. 'You are! Not getting mixed up in anything with my mother coming. Better go and tell Maria and Lady C the glad news, I suppose.'

'Give Leonora my love!' the earl said, and strolled off into the rain.

Mr. Rochford arrived a moment or two after the ladies

had returned from their shopping. He found them shaking the wet from their bonnets with exclamations of distress.

'Ruined!' Lady Constance said tragically, dabbing at her feathers. 'The curl has quite gone out of them! I declare there never was such a dreadful spring! Nothing but rain, rain, rain. Just from the shop to the barouche,' she said, holding it out to Mr. Rochford. 'The wretched coachman forgot to bring an umbrella.'

Mr. Rochford bowed over her hand, bonnet and all, and saluted Maria's cheek. She smiled up at him shyly. 'We didn't look to see you until this evening.'

'Wasn't coming until this evening, but I've had some bad news. Thought I'd better tell you as soon as I could.'

Leonora looked up quickly, her amber eyes overlarge in her face. 'Not . . .' she bit it off quickly. 'What news?'

'My mother's coming,' Mr. Rochford said heavily.

Leonora's lip curled. 'To look us over?'

Lady Constance directed a look that should have shrivelled her where she stood.

'But we were expecting your dear mama,' she told Mr. Rochford brightly. 'Naturally, she will wish to make Maria's acquaintance, and I daresay she has forgot that we used to know one another when we were young.' She smiled slightly. The Lady Constance Winton had always taken precedence over plain Miss Mary Webberly, even if she had married one of the richest men in the county. 'In fact I was wishing to meet her soon, for I am planning to give a little party when you make your announcement, and we must get together over the lists.'

Mr. Rochford's heart sank. He had envisaged a quiet wedding, attended by a few close friends, then a honeymoon abroad to escape the congratulations. It now struck him for the first time that the bride's mother had different ideas on how it should be done.

Before he could collect his wits the front-door knocker went again, and Mr. Barnethorpe erupted in, adding his share of water to that already on the marble floor, and depositing the rain from the brim of his beaver down Mr. Rochford's cambric shirt.

Mr. Rochford said apologetically, 'I daresay he wants to see Simon. I'll take him into the library out of the way.'

'Oh dear, I never offered any refreshment,' Lady Constance said worriedly when they had gone. 'Leonora, slip and tell Wilkins to attend to them.'

But Wilkins was somewhere in the depths, draping pelisses and greatcoats out to dry, so Leonora trod along the passage to the library in his stead. She was halfway there when Mr. Barnethorpe's ebullient tones arrested her.

'I was there smack on the dot when I acted for Millington! Trouble with Everard, he thinks only you Corinthian types can get up in the morning!'

'Well, he ain't asked you to be his second!' Mr. Rochford said irritably. 'And don't go blabbing all over the town. Cause more trouble than Finchley has before you're through! Everard can look after his own affairs, and he don't need your assistance. Beats me how you ever got elected to White's!'

Leonora stood, indignant thoughts jostling through her head. Seconds! Everard and Finchley! Lord Everard was proposing to fight a duel then. She had little opinion of duelling; even less when one of the contestants was a notoriously poor shot and the other was famed through London for his marksmanship. It would be little better than plain murder if this was the method Lord Everard had chosen to solve his problem.

She returned to the hall and gave the bell such a tug that it brought out not only Wilkins but the butler as well, then went to pen a second letter to the earl. Attended by none of the heartburnings of the first, it was written and sealed in a trice, and she awaited the results impatiently.

As it turned out, the letter did not come to the earl's hands until the following morning, by which time he was fully engaged for the day. It was therefore the day after before he presented himself in response to Leonora's summons, and by then her feelings were mixed. Her first triumphant indignation had abated, but she had declined an expedition in case he should call while she was out. When the others returned, full of their pleasurable morning, she perversely held the earl responsible for her loss of enjoyment, and when she stayed home in the afternoon, and still he did not come, she began to simmer again.

One glance was sufficient to inform the earl that his beloved's feelings were disturbed. Bowing over her hand, he murmured, 'I did not receive your note until yesterday.'

Leonora shot a quick glance at Lady Constance, who was hovering at the foot of the stairs, and led him into the front room. 'Mama might have heard you!'

'You have been indiscreet,' the earl said agreeably. 'Did you have to bribe the footman?'

'No, I did not—and I did not ask you to call to discuss my indiscretions, but your own dishonourable behaviour!'

'Leonora, you're becoming pious again,' the earl said resignedly.

Leonora gasped. 'I! Pious!'

'Pious,' he repeated firmly. 'What am I supposed to have done this time?'

'You must be totally lacking in conscience if you don't know,' Leonora said acidly. 'Possibly it slipped your mind amongst your other activities, but I was referring to your intention to fight a duel with Sir Mark. Whatever he may have done, the original fault was yours. No doubt I imbibed some unfashionable ideas in the country, but to challenge him to a duel when you are so much the better shot is utterly despicable!'

'You behold a broken man,' the earl said profoundly. 'I thought you might have sent for me out of concern for my own welfare. Now I find you still cherish tender feelings for Sir Mark!'

Leonora blushed fierily. 'I do not!'

'I was informed that you once contemplated marriage with him!'

'You were informed wrongly!'

'And so were you,' the earl returned. 'Who told you I had challenged Finchley?'

'I am not at liberty to tell you, but I assure you it was from a completely reliable source.'

'Leonora, you've been eavesdropping!' He saw the colour creep up her cheeks again, and grinned.

She said stiffly, 'I did not give you leave to use my name.'

'Very well. For your information, madam, I have not challenged Finchley to a duel. My chief concern has been to avoid one. I am possessed of some unfashionable notions myself. I even pay the tradesmen!'

'Oh,' Leonora said, a little uncertainly. She sat down by the table and leaned her chin on her hands. 'Why is it so difficult to avoid?'

'Think, my little one. Put yourself in my place. Finchley is spreading this story, and it is known that it has come to my ears. What would an innocent man do?'

'Couldn't you fire into the air?'

'How heroic! I see you read novels as well. Tell me, do you understand the significance of such a course?'

'No,' Leonora confessed.

'And hasn't it occurred to you that if I carried out this dastardly plot to rid myself of Finchley, I should be forced to flee the country?'

'No,' Leonora repeated, the wind taken out of her sails.

The informality creeping back into their exchange was not lost upon the earl, and, smiling, he seated himself on the opposite side of the table.

'To fire into the air would be to acknowledge myself guilty. No—I shall have to administer a minor flesh wound.'

'But can you be sure of doing that?'

'Of course not. And he might even hit me. He did once, after all.' He watched carefully for the results of this calculated speech, and thought he detected a shade of anxiety.

She stood up. 'Perhaps it won't come to that.'

'Perhaps it won't,' the earl agreed, politely rising to his feet also.

Leonora faced him doubtfully. She knew not how, but they seemed to be on terms of amity again, and she was uncertain how to proceed. Finally, she asked if he would care for a glass of sherry, and preserving his countenance with difficulty, the earl accepted. They waited in silence until Wilkins entered with the tray, and then, since his beloved seemed to have lost her normally active tongue, the earl asked if she was attending the assembly at Almack's on the following Wednesday.

'Yes, Lady Jersey sent us vouchers. At least,' she checked, 'Mrs. Rochford is coming to town, but I expect we shall still be going.'

'Mrs. Rochford does have the entrée to Almack's,' the earl agreed, straight-faced.

'Of course she does! She's as thick as thieves with the Princess Esterhazy. That isn't what I meant, as well you know! The thing is, Mama intends giving an engagement party, and if they get wrapped up in wedding arrangements, one never knows what may happen.'

'I see I had a very narrow escape,' the earl murmured, risking everything, 'though I don't have a mama to complicate the arrangements.'

'I didn't know.'

'There are a lot of things about me that you don't know.'

He strolled over to the window and drew back the net curtains. 'We appear to have a brief burst of sunshine. If you were to have that traffic-shy grey saddled, I could give you my entire life history as we circled the park.'

Leonora hesitated, the memory of their previous ride still sharp, then nodded. 'Very well. Give me half an hour.'

'Half an hour may be sufficient for you, but I have to get home as well.' He lifted her chin with a forefinger. 'I thought for a moment you were going to show craven.'

She stared defiantly up at him. 'Three-quarters then!'

He nodded agreement. 'And don't neglect to inform your mama. It should cast her into transports!'

It was regrettable, but Leonora found he was right.

Lady Constance, after eyeing her warily, formed the opinion that her daughter's frame of mind had mellowed and uttered clucks of delight.

'For to be honest, after your conduct at the theatre, I thought you must have quite ruined your chances!'

Leonora's chin went up, but with the memory of Lord Everard's parting remark, her sense of humour reasserted itself, and she was still quite in charity with him as they set out down the road.

'How did Lady Constance react?' he enquired.

'She positively twittered,' Leonora admitted. 'I can't imagine how you contrive to be so well thought of. You have half the mamas in London fawning at your feet. Did they but know what I do,' she added pensively.

The earl grinned. 'An eminently practical woman, your mama. I'm quite a catch, you know.'

'Well, she may abandon this notion at the outset, for we don't share the same views!'

'You're not likely to receive a better offer,' the earl told her, apparently unwounded. 'Dukes and marquises are thin on the ground.'

'There are other considerations besides worldly ones,' Leonora said loftily.

'I know there are, but I thought I was quite personable! Were you thinking of becoming Mrs. Eccleston, I should seriously consider the disparity in height. Imagine the appearance you must present going down the aisle.' Leonora gave him a withering look, and he continued musingly: 'Or perhaps Mrs. Denston? A pleasant enough man, comfortably situated, but a trifle lacking in character, don't you think? No personality!'

His summing up of the worthy Mr. Denston was sufficiently accurate to dispel any faint leanings Leonora may have felt towards him, and her resentment increased.

'Let me inform you, sir, that matrimony is not my sole aim in life!'

'Ah.' The earl's tone was warmly sympathetic. 'You are resolved on a life of spinsterhood. You wish to devote yourself to good works and charitable causes.'

'No, I do not!' Leonora snapped. 'At least, I think one should do what one can to help people less fortunately circumstanced, but I don't think it's at all necessary to eschew society or retire to a nunnery in order to do it!'

'Then what do you want?' Lord Everard enquired reasonably. 'Mr. Eccleston has not enough height for you, the amiable Denston not enough personality, and yet you are not resolved to remain unwed. Without undue conceit, I feel I have the advantage over both gentlemen. While I confess that I may not conform to the ideal, where do I fall so sadly short?'

Searching madly through her brain for any obvious deficiencies of character, Leonora was forced to fall back on feminine illogicality. 'Mainly that I cannot be half an hour in your company without falling out with you,' she snapped. 'Everything I say, you twist into a meaning I never intended. Besides,' she added, as a theme suggested itself, 'we have nothing in common. Your whole life is the clubs and sporting circle, and the social set.'

The earl forbore to remark that her own life seemed mainly to be composed of expeditions of pleasure, and merely said hopefully, 'You're perfectly right. You don't think you might like to reform me?'

Leonora looked up and discovered he was laughing at her. A reluctant smile dawned in response. 'I have enough sense not to attempt the impossible. Let's canter while we still have the room. This sunshine is sure to bring everyone out.' She gathered the grey up and sent him on, and the earl watched for a moment before catching her up.

'What other accomplishments have you?'

'Not many,' Leonora admitted, 'though you needn't make it sound as though I only had the one. I am told that my performance on the pianoforte is above average, and my paintings,' she said, straight-faced, 'are much admired by my family.'

'You must let me have an example of each so that I may judge. And talking of family, you have conjured a member up!' He pointed with his riding whip, and Leonora beheld her brother, not only attired with unusual propriety but bending his head attentively towards a young lady on his arm.

'Good gracious! Simon with a girl!' Leonora exclaimed. 'Who on earth is she?'

'Unless I mistake the matter,' the earl said, studying the half-averted profile, 'it is none other than my ward!'

'Of course! I met her for a moment at the theatre!' She waved a greeting, and the couple paused until she was alongside.

'Lady Sarah! How do you do.'

It struck her that her brother was looking a little conscious, and Lord Everard, who had dismounted and was walking by his ward, was wearing an expression of unholy amusement.

'What a pity we didn't know what you intended,' he drawled. 'We could have formed a party. I haven't ridden out with Sarah since before Christmas!'

'Lady Everard gave her permission, sir,' Simon said quickly.

The earl glanced at him. 'I'm sure she did,' he said drily.

Leonora's gaze flickered from one to the other in quick puzzlement, but the earl had turned away, and was leading them along one of the paths back towards the gate. She commanded her brother to help her down so that she could talk to Lady Sarah, and walked on her other side, chatting easily of fashions and the dreadful weather.

Some of Sarah's constraint and stiffness disappeared, and when she smiled, as she did frequently at Simon, it lit up her face, transforming it from ordinary prettiness to something quite lovely. Her pale hair was framed by an olive-green bonnet, and her green pelisse was well cut and elegant. In her manner she was obviously unsure of herself, but she was talking easily enough now, in her light, pleasant voice, and altogether Leonora found her most presentable. She was aware of the type of female her graceless brother had previously consorted with. If Sarah was his more serious choice, then she had no fault to find with it.

When they met up with Lady Constance's barouche on the main carriageway by the gates she was thus unprepared for the expression of ludicrous dismay which crossed her mama's face, or for her manner, which, while it was civil, could never be described as enthusiastic.

8

The weather broke up the company before she could satisfy her curiosity. The heavens opened, and in the face of the sudden downpour Lady Constance could do nothing but scramble Sarah into the coach, while the chivalrous Mr. Rochford was thrust out into the wet to make room for her.

He and Simon made what speed was consistent with dignity to where they might hope to pick up a hackney, while the earl, thoroughly entertained by Lady Constance's dilemma, threw Leonora up into the saddle.

They clattered through the streets, and the earl remarked conversationally that he seemed to remember having done it before.

'I wasn't wearing my best riding habit then,' Leonora said crisply, refusing to give way to nostalgia. 'Thank goodness we're nearly home!'

As they drew level with the house, the earl reached out and put a restraining hand on her bridle. 'Give him to me and I'll take him round to the mews. You go straight in.'

She thanked him and fled up the stairs, her emotions once more confused. Each time she decided she now had her feelings firmly under control, he undermined her by some small remark or gesture.

As she rang the bell, she told herself that any gentleman must have done the same under the circumstances; witness poor Mr. Rochford, drenched through his gallantry. But her mind's eye treacherously recalled the earl's warm smile as he took her horse, and, try as she might, she could not convince herself that it had been merely an act of courtesy.

She continued her argument as she changed into a dry gown, searching for some fault on which she could centre her feelings. He was indolent, of course. In common with most of the fashionable world, he seemed to have no thoughts that were not connected with his own entertainment.

Bred in the country, Leonora had been brought up with the acceptance of responsibility towards those living on the estate. While they froze in Revell House, the villagers still had the right to collect their fuel from the woods, and Lady Constance, distraught with her economies at home, concerned herself with the sick and aged, and made practical contributions to assist them.

The earl, as far as she could see, did nothing, and she managed to work herself up into quite a frenzy of righteous indignation. Such people were nothing but parasites on the face of the earth!

Encountering Mr. Rochford in the drawing room, she expressed her thoughts verbally, and the hapless Mr. Rochford was startled to find himself, as well as the earl, under attack.

'Nothing to do with me!' he protested. 'Corn Laws are shocking, of course, but I didn't make 'em. Not a peer, and not a member of parliament!'

'Lord Everard is!'

'A member of parliament?'

'No, of course not, but he's a peer, so *he* could do something!"

'I suppose so,' Mr. Rochford said, eyeing her queerly, 'but I should dashed well think he's done enough!' Rendered brave in defence of the earl, he added, 'Spent a fortune on Abbotsford, or a good part of his anyway, on putting the lands to rights!'

'Oh,' Leonora said, a trifle disconcerted. 'Well, I expect it was only so that it should run profitably.'

'It was not,' Mr. Rochford retorted, nettled. 'Be years before he sees his money back! Told him so myself!'

Leonora reviewed this in her mind for a moment. 'I didn't know, but on the other hand, if you have the money, it is nothing terribly arduous merely to direct your steward how to spend it.'

'Direct!' Mr. Rochford spluttered. 'I don't know why you've got this opinion of Louis, but I can tell you that he rode over every dashed field and inspected every farm and cottage and barn on the place!'

'How do you know?' Leonora said waveringly.

'Because I was dashed well with him!' Mr. Rochford said with bitterness, remembering the acres of fields they had ploughed through, their horses up to their knees in mud and water. 'It strikes me you've got the wrong notion of Louis altogether. He's a very good sort of fellow!'

'I'm sure he must be,' Leonora said, a trifle hollowly. It came hard to discover that the earl was also an excellent landlord. For a moment she wondered if she had made a dreadful mistake in his motives. He seemed to have so many admirable qualities, and except for the situations arising out of his flirtations, no one had a word to say in his disparagement. It was here that a small voice in her brain began to list the damsels his name had been associated with. Catherine Harford's disposition might count against her, but there were others who combined birth and fortune with quite a degree of beauty.

Subjecting herself to a critical analysis, Leonora concluded that she was woefully lacking in what a highly eligible nobleman would look for in a wife. Through Lady Constance, her connections were respectable, but certainly not enough to make her sought after. Her dowry was negligible, and her conduct was frequently censured by her mama as unbecoming.

Drearily, she also came to the conclusion that she lacked the charm and beauty sufficient to make the earl propose marriage after such a short acquaintance. There must, therefore, be some other reason for his flattering offer.

Watched by the perplexed, but ever polite Mr. Rochford, she was dwelling on the earl's charm of manner, which made inexperienced young women lose their heads and fall in love at first sight, when her mama and Maria arrived.

As a tragic entrance it was unequalled, and quite put to shame a similar performance they had seen at the theatre the previous week. Casting her bonnet on to the table, Lady Constance sank into a convenient chair, and with half-closed eyes let out a shuddering moan.

'What on earth . . . ?' Leonora's eyes sought enlightenment from Maria, but she received only a shrug in reply. 'Mama, what has occurred?'

Lady Constance's lids fluttered, and she cast an

anguished glance heavenwards. Apparently deriving no comfort, she moaned weakly for her smelling salts.

'Not until I know what all this is about!' Leonora returned vigorously. She caught Mr. Rochford edging towards the door. His expression suggested that he knew something of the matter, and under her accusing gaze he faltered to a standstill.

'I rather think,' he said carefully, 'that she may have met Lady Everard.'

'Oh, the Dowager Countess.' Leonora's face cleared. 'But what of it?'

Between repeated murmurings of 'That woman,' Lady Constance was groping in her reticule.

Mr. Rochford surveyed her for a moment, then said helpfully, 'Often has that effect on people! M'mother don't recognise her!'

'Why ever not?' Leonora said, astonished.

Mr. Rochford's colour deepened slightly, from which Leonora deduced that it was a delicate matter. 'Lady Constance will tell you,' he muttered.

'My poor Simon!' Lady Constance said, in throbbing tones.

'Oh for heaven's sake!' Leonora said disgustedly. 'Maria, ring for some tea, and tell me what you know!'

'I really don't know anything. I didn't get out of the carriage. We took Lady Sarah home, and Mama escorted her in. Then, when she was coming out, she met Simon.'

'I thought Simon came with you,' Leonora said, turning to Mr. Rochford.

He shook his head. 'Wouldn't come in. Took the hackney on to see Lady Sarah.'

'Yes, very well. What happened then?'

'Mama said something to Simon, but I didn't hear what it was.'

'Heaven send me patience,' Leonora muttered. 'Did you hear what Simon said?'

'Oh yes,' Maria returned seriously. 'He said "Fustian".'

'To his own mother!' Lady Constance interposed dramatically.

Leonora's lip quivered. 'I suppose it was bound to happen. She hasn't had the vapours since we came to London! Am I to take it that Lady Everard, in some way, is not respectable?'

'Respectable! We all saw her at the theatre with that dreadful man, but when I went in to restore her daughter to her he was there in the house! Obviously quite at home too! And if she had any relation in the house to bear her company, it was more than I could discover! How can she or that daughter ever hope to be accepted? And when I ventured to hint as much to Simon, he said . . .'

'Fustian!' Leonora supplied. 'All very dreadful, I daresay, but is it really of such great moment? Look at Lady Oxford with all her various children! And Lady Bessborough was still being received when I last heard her mentioned.'

'Leonora!' Lady Constance exclaimed, deeply shocked, 'Mr. Rochford . . .'

Exasperated, Leonora said, 'Mama, don't be ridiculous! Paul is shortly going to be one of the family, and if he imagines that Maria and I don't hear any of the stories that are going about, he must suppose us to be simpleminded!'

Lady Constance, undecided whether to have a spasm, or acknowledge the truth of Leonora's speech, said feebly, 'The two cases are not the same. Don't ask me why, but it is so. Lady Oxford has been a leading hostess for years, and Lady Everard hasn't. Why, look what happened only recently when they tried to re-establish Byron and his sister after that appalling scandal. Complete disaster!'

'I really don't see why Lady Everard's conduct should affect Sarah, though,' Leonora said. 'She has done nothing, after all, and she's the daughter of the late earl, and Everard's cousin.'

'It is by no means of the same consequence to be only the cousin of the present earl,' Lady Constance said. 'Nothing in the world could get her admitted to Almack's! She will find herself completely ostracised by everyone who matters, and she hasn't even a decent dowry to recommend her, from what I've heard.'

'She's still Lord Everard's ward,' Leonora argued. 'And he will surely provide her with a reasonable portion. Don't you think so?' She turned enquiringly to Mr. Rochford, who nodded.

'Very true what Lady Constance says, though. Awkward situation.'

'Everyone is behaving as though he had made her an offer,' Leonora said bracingly. 'It cannot be so serious for him merely to take her walking in the park. I have done so with quite a few men, and I'm not yet married to any of them. If no one makes a fuss to Simon, it will probably blow over.'

'Not by the way he spoke to me!' Lady Constance said, in depressed tones. 'And you may depend on it, the mother will do anything she can to get the girl married and out of the way. And Simon is of full age,' she concluded mournfully.

'Can nothing be done?' Leonora asked Mr. Rochford.

'Might be, if Everard could get someone to take Lady Sarah on,' he said, after consideration. 'Can't think of anyone who would, though.'

'Couldn't you speak to Lord Everard?' Leonora persisted, but Mr. Rochford stared at her in utter horror, lost for a reply. 'Oh well, let us not cross bridges before we come to them, but simply wait and see what occurs.'

The subject was allowed to drop, but if Lady Constance cherished hopes that her words of warning might be heeded, she was to be disappointed. Simon's spotted handkerchief disappeared, to be replaced by modest, if inexpertly tied neckcloths. He no longer came home in the small hours in a state of inebriation, and the promising liaison with the attractive blonde ended before it was begun.

The only thing he would not do was inform his fond mother where he now spent his time. When she ventured a tentative enquiry, he spoke darkly of some snug little lodgings he had been to see. The immediate effect of this was to send her hot foot upstairs to write a letter informing Mr. Revell that his son and heir was embarked on a course ruinous to both himself and his family, and it was a father's duty to come up to town and exert his authority before it was too late.

To Leonora, Simon merely said there was no pleasing his mother. When he used to kick up a few larks with his friends he had to endure lectures on depravity and the error of his ways; now he was reformed, and as sober as any parent could wish, she was screeching that he was on the road to ruin.

'It is only because of her concern for you,' Leonora pointed out. 'And if you don't wish to be lectured at breakfast, you'd better take it where you have all your other meals. It's the only opportunity she has to speak to you nowadays.'

'You sound like Mama,' Simon said, hunching his shoulders.

'She's disappointed. She hoped, I suppose, that you would make a good match that would help the estate. Myself,' Leonora said, wrinkling her nose with sisterly candour, 'I shouldn't have thought you had enough address to bowl over an heiress. And I wouldn't call Revell House a lure!'

'You ain't seen it recently!' Simon said, momentarily diverted. 'The old man has been setting it all to rights, and when the money starts coming in from the new land it's going to be a very decent property. We shan't be quite the poor relations that we were!'

'You mean Aunt Margaret. All the more reason for Mama to want you to make a good marriage. You can't expect her to be cast into transports at the prospect of a connection with Lady Everard and Digby!'

'There's no need for her to have anything to do with them. I don't like Lady Everard myself. She doesn't care what becomes of Sarah really. Just wants her married and off her hands. But Sarah isn't like her mother, and if only Mama would get to know her, she'd realise it.'

Leonora sat quietly for a moment, a little touched by the new seriousness in her brother. In a few days he had changed from an irresponsible young man without a thought in his head except cockfighting and horses, and the riotous revels with his friends. Suddenly she could picture him as he would be in the future, with a wife and children, thoughtful of their welfare.

'You want to marry Sarah.' It was a statement rather than a question. Simon nodded, and she sighed. 'You think Mama is being unjust and making Sarah suffer for something that is no fault of hers, and Mama thinks you have no idea of the consequences of what you are doing. And the trouble is,' she continued with another sigh, 'you are both of you right.'

'I'm not interested in this social life Mama thinks so highly of!'

'Sarah may be!'

'She isn't!'

'How do you know?' Leonora said. 'She might, from pride, say she doesn't care for balls and assemblies, but you don't know what she really thinks. The truth is that she's unlikely to receive a better offer, and it may be that she feels marriage with you would at least bring about an improvement in her position!'

Simon said vehemently, 'It's nothing like that at all! You none of you know her!'

Leonora admitted this was true. She added, 'You know of course, that Papa has been sent for, and will probably arrive today.'

In fact, Lady Constance fell on his neck not three hours later. Unable to judge the situation from a distance of two counties, Mr. Revell had posted up immediately.

Restraining herself long enough to ask if he had breakfasted, Lady Constance dragged him into the front saloon and poured her troubles into his ears. It took some time, with facts and opinions inextricably mixed together, and she was obliged, on several occasions, to resort to her handkerchief.

Mr. Revell heard her patiently, and took a pinch of snuff while he considered it. Resting his foot on the hearth, he said finally, 'What is it you wish me to do?'

Lady Constance stared at him. 'Why, stop him!'

'How? Disinherit him? Stop his allowance?'

'Reason with him! Tell him he mustn't!'

'Thank you! I am to tell a young man of twenty-three, in love for the first time, that he mustn't! If he has an ounce of red blood in his veins, I know what he will tell me in reply!'

Lady Constance looked at him aghast. For several days she had been regarding Mr. Revell's return as the magical cure for her troubles. 'But he must listen to his own father!'

Mr. Revell said drily, 'I suspect, my dear, that he may already have heard too much from his own mother. Certainly I can threaten to disinherit him or stop his allowance, but he's a grown man and will very likely tell me to go to the devil. Who do I leave Revell House to then? Who helps me to run the estate?'

Lady Constance stared into the fire, tears trickling slowly down her cheeks. 'So there is nothing we can do?'

Mr. Revell patted her on the shoulder. 'I don't think it is as bad as you make out. The girl can't be portionless if she's Everard's ward, and though I don't doubt there will be some embarrassment, it won't greatly affect you and the girls. As long as there is nothing you dislike in Sarah herself, for Simon's sake I should make the best of it.' He raised his bushy brows. 'And there is always the possibility that he may fall out of love again next week.'

'Everard's ward!' Lady Constance exclaimed, clutching his arm. 'Of course she is! Simon must apply to him for consent! He may refuse!'

'My dear, there is no reason why he should. As things stand, he must be glad to receive any offer at all. Where is Simon, by the way?'

'I don't know, but I can guess,' Lady Constance said hollowly. 'Except for breakfast, we don't see him in the house. I asked the other day where he was spending his time, but he threatened to go into lodgings, so I haven't dared mention it since.' Her tears began to flow afresh.

'I'll have a word with him when he comes in. Until then I should put it out of your mind.' He settled himself into a chair by the fire. 'How are the girls?'

Lady Constance mopped her eyes and brightened a little. 'Dear Paul is looking for a town house. They will fix the date of the wedding as soon as he finds one which is suitable.' Becoming more animated, she said, 'Mrs. Rochford was due to come to London last week, but her daughter produced unexpectedly. A son at her first! They must be thrilled! I was hoping to fix the date for a little party, but I daresay she will be with us in a few days.'

'And Leonora?' Mr. Revell said.

'Oh dear, I don't know what has got into the girl,' Lady Constance sighed. 'Lord Everard was becoming quite particular in his attentions. Not merely flirting, I'm certain, but would you believe it, Leonora will have none of him. I'm sure I don't know what she expects—a more pleasant man would be hard to find. She can't afford to be so contrary. I've told her so many times, but she never would heed me.'

'Leave her alone,' Mr. Revell advised. 'I don't know what she's about any more than you do, but no good will come from meddling.'

Lady Constance looked doubtful, but had to be content.

Since Simon, as foretold, no longer returned to the parental home for meals, and his changes of raiment seemed to be accomplished when they were engaged elsewhere, Mr. Revell lay in wait for him that night.

With a branch of candles nearby, he arranged himself comfortably by a snug fire, and spread his steward's books around him so that he might continue checking the figures, an occupation Lady Constance's impassioned appeal had interrupted.

A little after eleven the porter answered the door, and Mr. Revell strolled out into the hall.

Simon stiffened when he saw him. 'I didn't know you were here, sir!'

'You knew damn well your mother had sent for me, though,' Mr. Revell said. 'Come in here. If I'm to judge the matter, I'd like both versions.' He resumed his seat by the fire. 'Pass the decanter. You seem agreeably sober, so we might as well share it!'

Simon grinned. 'It seems my mother don't care any more for me sober than she did before!'

'Very likely,' Mr. Revell said agreeably. 'She hasn't considered the virtues of the matter as well as its drawbacks.' He waited until Simon had filled his glass, and, eyeing his son reflectively, said, 'We'll have some straight answers. Do you intend to marry Sarah Matheson?'

'I haven't asked her, sir, but yes, I do!'

'And you've considered it from all sides. Her father wasn't at all well thought of, and you probably know better than I what's said of her mother.'

'Yes, and Sarah feels it more than anyone!' Simon said hotly.

'No need to fly up at me. I'm stating facts.'

'My mother makes too much of them. Sarah is Lord Everard's ward, and Mama can't very well say *he* ain't respectable!'

'Precisely what I told her,' Mr. Revell nodded. 'I don't see what we can do about it for the present, but meantime there's no need to treat this house as though we had a case of the plague.'

Simon pulled a wry face. 'You don't know Mama!'

'On the contrary, my boy, I know her a good deal better than you do,' Mr. Revell said genially. 'You leave her to me. Meanwhile, we might as well finish the decanter. They won't be home for hours yet!'

What he said to Lady Constance, Simon was not privileged to know, but it had the effect of easing the atmosphere. Lady Constance sighed, and looked her sorrow, but stopped short at mentioning it further. For which, Simon confided to Mr. Rochford, he was profoundly thankful. 'I daresay my father don't like it any better than she does,' he added, 'but at least he understands it's the sort of thing a fellow has to make his own mind up about. And my mind is made up!'

Correctly interpreting that his role was meant to be that of go-between, Mr. Rochford dutifully repeated it to the earl at the first opportunity.

'The devil it is!' the earl exclaimed. 'That's sure to have cast Lady Constance into a rare flutter!'

'Can't expect them to like it,' Mr. Rochford said. 'The old man don't say anything, but I don't suppose it exactly has his blessing. Must have been a rum pair, your cousin and his wife.'

'They were,' the earl agreed. "So I am to receive a request for her hand from Simon! I shall have to see if I can do something about it!'

'What can you do?'

'I could set Sarah up in an establishment of her own, with some respectable female to act as chaperone. The trouble is,' he mused, 'that by now everyone is watching them. If I could get rid of Caroline, it wouldn't present such a particular appearance. If I remove Sarah while her mother's still living in town, I'm afraid it might not serve —the reason for doing it is too obvious. I shall have to have another go at Caroline. I fear that this time I may be forced to do something disagreeable, like offering to withdraw my . . . er, monetary assistance.'

'Might work the trick,' Mr. Rochford opined. 'Digby ain't too well breeched from what I've heard.'

'All the better. In the meantime, you may assure Simon that the matter is receiving my fullest attention.'

'Nothing to do with me!' Mr. Rochford said hurriedly.

9

The following week the worry of Simon was driven from Lady Constance's mind. Mrs. Rochford arrived in town, and paid a morning call at once.

'Constance!' she cried, offering a scented cheek, 'I declare I should have known you anywhere! You haven't changed in the least!'

Offering a cheek in return, Lady Constance tried confusedly to remember whether they had ever been on such close terms before, and said she would also have known her dearest Mary anywhere; after which both ladies stood back and took stock of one another.

Mrs. Rochford, Lady Constance thought, had become atrociously dowdy, even though she must be some forty-eight years old by now, while Mrs. Rochford satisfied herself with the thought that she had always known Constance Winton would run to fat.

She followed her into the drawing room, exclaiming that she could hardly wait to meet Maria. 'Nothing but Elizabeth's confinement could have kept me away, I assure you. So vexatious! She was not due until the end of the month, but everything went splendidly. A fine boy, and she is so well that I have not the least scruple in leaving her now. Her old nanny has her in charge, and I can rely on her utterly.'

Slightly buffeted, Lady Constance murmured a few agreeable phrases, and directed that her daughters should be summoned. Relieved to find Mrs. Rochford apparently well disposed toward the match, she had no fear that Maria would let her down. Though she was still quiet, their sojourn in London had perfected her company manners, and her beauty was undeniable. Unless Mrs. Rochford wanted a prattle-box, she could have no fault to find with her. Lady Constance hoped fervently, however, that Leonora would hold her tongue. Notwithstanding her present affability, Mrs. Rochford could be as stiff as any of the patronesses of Almack's, and she was a stickler for the proprieties.

Leonora, however, had a real affection for Mr. Rochford, and was resolved to be at her most saintly with his mother. Since it was Maria with whom Mrs. Rochford was most concerned, she was at pains to efface herself, only taking part in the conversation when she was directly addressed, and behaving throughout with a quiet elegance of manner, which, irrationally, aroused in Lady Constance a strong desire to box her ears when she thought of all the times when her daughter's conduct had put her to the blush.

All went very well. It was obvious that Mrs. Rochford was genuinely pleased with Maria, and Lady Constance outlined her plan of giving a party to honour the engagement now it was to be officially announced.

'It cannot be a very large affair,' she was explaining, 'for the ballroom here is not as big as I could wish. We have made so many friends that the problem is going to be whom we shall have to leave out.'

Mrs. Rochford agreed it was a problem. 'But you will be inviting the Princess Esterhazy, and Countess Lieven, of course, and dear Emily Cowper.'

Lady Constance gulped. Left to herself, she very much doubted whether she would, but hearing them so casually referred to gave her the courage to agree that on no account must they be left out. 'And, of course, my sister Margaret. She was a particular friend of yours, I remember.' Never did she think she would have the cause to be grateful for Margaret's odious self-consequence, but she admitted to herself that it gave her a certain exhilaration to be able to claim a noted member of the *ton* on her own account. It was then that a devastating thought struck her, affecting her so powerfully that she faltered in her reply to Mrs. Rochford. Observing closely from her corner, Leonora formed the opinion that her Mama's mind was no longer wholly concerned with the matter in hand.

As soon as they were alone, she pounced, demanding to know the reason for her abstraction.

'Oh, Leonora,' Lady Constance said, wringing her hands. 'The most dreadful thought came to me! Simon will expect me to invite Sarah, I know he will! It has completely destroyed all my pleasure, and I was so looking forward to giving our first party.'

'I do see what you mean,' Leonora admitted. 'It is bound to be a trifle awkward. Need you invite her?'

'Simon would never forgive me if I didn't, and your father says I must accept that he means to marry her if I don't wish for a break.'

Leonora leaned her chin on her hands to consider the problem. 'You will have to make the best of it, I suppose. Sarah herself is quite unexceptionable.'

'I know she is,' Lady Constance wailed. 'But you can't have considered! How can I invite Sarah without asking Lady Everard as well? And you heard Mrs. Rochford. We're to have the Princess Esterhazy and heaven knows how many other of the patronesses of Almack's, as well as your Aunt Margaret. Can you imagine it when they find themselves in the same room as that woman!' She clasped her hands together as a ray of hope struck her. 'How long is it since Lord Everard died?'

'It must be six months by now, and they're certainly not *wearing* mourning.'

'How dreadful! It's worse than ever!' Lady Constance said agitatedly. 'They're perfectly capable of coming in something completely outrageous!'

'Leave it to me,' Leonora said suddenly, pursuing her own line of thought. 'I may be able to do something.'

Thus it was that the next time Lord Everard called in his phaeton to take her driving he found his invitation accepted with surprising alacrity. Unable to leave well alone, he murmured a comment.

'I daresay you are surprised, but I want to talk to you,' Leonora said, with unsettling honesty. 'Is your groom with you?'

'Yes,' the earl admitted, 'but if it is private, we can always stroll hand in hand amongst the primroses.'

A gurgle of laughter escaped Leonora. 'How ridiculous! But I'm afraid we shall have to. It's not at all the sort of thing we could discuss in front of him.'

Accordingly, they went further afield than usual, and

when they reached a suitable spot the earl handed her down.

'Now,' he said, when they were side by side, 'what is it that you want me to do?'

'How unhandsome!' Leonora exclaimed. 'I merely want the benefit of your advice.'

'I mistrust you. Carry on.'

'You may or may not be aware that my brother has fallen desperately in love with your ward, and wishes to marry her!'

'He has not yet applied to me, but I did have an inkling!'

'I suppose that is what you were laughing at the day we all met together,' Leonora said accusingly.

'The humour of the situation did strike me.'

'Well, it doesn't strike Mama,' Leonora returned tartly. 'The thing is, she is giving a party for Maria and Paul, and she's at her wit's end. Mrs. Rochford has taken a hand in it, and half the snobs in town are likely to be present. You can just imagine the reaction there would be to Lady Everard!'

'Is it Sarah or merely my revered cousin Caroline that your mother objects to?'

Leonora looked at him doubtfully. 'I'm sorry. It must appear very rude of me to be discussing your relatives like this.'

'Not at all,' the earl said politely. He marred his reply somewhat by adding, 'I'm storing it up in case I should ever wish to speak disparagingly of your inarticulate sister.'

'How odious of you! No, Mama, I think, is quite resigned to Lady Sarah, though obviously she doesn't *wish*

Simon to ally himself with a girl who isn't received. I do apologise! It sounds dreadful to put into words, but if we're to discuss it at all I have to.'

'Don't spare my feelings or we shall never get to the crux of the matter,' the earl said. 'You want me, I take it, to find a way out of this dilemma.'

'You don't think the circumstance of their being in mourning forbids it?' Leonora said hopefully.

'It certainly wouldn't forbid the countess!"

'No. Which makes one think your cousin must have been a rather disagreeable man.'

'Very disagreeable. Shall we turn back? You will get your shoes muddy if we go any further down here.' They retraced their steps in silence while the earl thought the matter over. Finally, his eyes glinting down at her, he said, 'May I enquire whether I am to be invited to this romp?'

'Of course! You are Paul's oldest friend!'

'In which case, you may leave it in my hands. Issue the invitations quite normally, and I will engage for Lady Everard's being unable to attend. I shall then, quite properly, escort my ward in her stead. Will that set your mama's mind at rest?'

'Thank you!' Leonora said radiantly. 'I knew you would find a way. I'll tell Mama as soon as . . .' She broke off, and the earl grinned.

'Quite so. All you have to do now is think up a convincing reason for why you were discussing it with me in the first place.'

'I don't suppose you could think of one?'

'No, my little one, I can't. Your best course probably is to confess, and hope your mama doesn't notice in the midst of her relief.'

'You're perfectly right,' Leonora said, much struck. 'Provided I don't mention that you inveigled me into accompanying you down a deserted country lane, out of sight of your groom, I shall have nothing to fear.'

'Inveigled?' the earl said, lifting an eyebrow.

'Certainly!'

They strolled back to the phaeton in agreeable silence until Leonora said curiously, 'How will you prevent Lady Everard from attending?'

'That, madam, is no concern of yours,' the earl told her. 'When I make rash promises, however, I endeavour to keep them. Rest assured that if I can't prevent one, I shall prevent both!'

Feeling that there was no time like the present for getting unpleasant things done, he called on the countess later that morning. Ushered into the drawing room by her superior butler, he occupied himself with examining the ornaments until Caroline joined him.

'Pricing them, Louis?' she enquired caustically.

'Within my limited knowledge,' the earl admitted, replacing a bronze statuette on the shelf. 'I imagine your protector is feeling the pinch by now. Rumour has it that the unfortunate financial state of the country is affecting him.'

'I never listen to rumours,' the countess said indifferently.

'How agreeable for you. Is my ward home—or is she being squired by young Revell?'

'Since you ask, I believe she is.'

'My dear Caroline, I cannot help feeling that you are

being somewhat lax in the performance of your maternal duties. May I sit down? This is going to take some time.'

'You may as well. I take it that it is my maternal duties you have come to discuss.'

'That and your financial affairs,' the earl agreed.

The countess stood up and paced the room. 'Then for your information I consider that I performed my share of duty when I stayed with Robert until he died. If it hadn't been for Sarah, I should have left him sixteen years ago.' She tapped a finger irritably on the shelf. 'But you know dear Robert. Being the man he was, he would never have let me keep Sarah if I'd left him.' Her lip curled. 'He'd have saddled himself with a daughter he didn't want just to spite me!'

'Believe me, I sympathise. But it strikes me that your sacrifice was in vain, if you're going to ruin her now. I fear I shall have to withdraw my financial support if you won't . . . er . . . conform.'

The countess regarded him for a moment, then smiled. 'If you do, there will be nothing for it but for my protector, as you term him, to move in here with me. It would be cheaper than running two establishments.'

'Masterly,' the earl acknowledged. 'That's holding me over a barrel. Tell me, why are you so averse to marriage? Don't you have the faintest yearnings towards respectability?'

She shrugged. 'It doesn't worry me. If I marry, I lose both my title and my allowance in one. Or had you forgotten the generous terms of my late husband's will?'

'I had,' the earl confessed. 'Look, Caroline, I've no desire to interfere in your private affairs, but I am responsible for Sarah. Her life is going to be affected if things continue as they are. We'll clear one point now, and discuss the larger issues afterwards.' He leaned back and placed his fingertips together.

'You cannot be so inattentive that you have failed to notice the situation developing between Sarah and young Revell.'

'Of course I've noticed,' the Countess said scornfully. 'I see no reason to be unduly concerned over Sarah when it's all likely to be resolved in a week or two.'

'There's a good deal of opposition to the match from his family!'

'Is there? And what's the father? Some country squire?'

'Don't dismiss them so derisively, Caroline. The younger daughter is about to announce her betrothal to Paul Rochford, which gives rise to a problem. Lady Constance is giving a party, to which she feels she must invite Sarah and yourself. And,' the earl said with a smile, 'you must admit that your presence at such a gathering is bound to be conducive of a certain embarrassment.'

'Don't let them put themselves about. I've no wish to go!'

'I didn't think you would, which is why I engaged to make your excuses and escort Sarah myself.'

'Did you,' the countess returned. 'Cool of you, without consulting me.'

'Wasn't it,' the earl agreed. 'But I shall require your co-operation. Sarah must be suitably attired in half-mourning —you will naturally send bills to me—and she must be coached in the behaviour expected of her. She will not take part in dancing or anything of the sort. Can I rely on you?'

'In this, yes you can.'

'Good! Now we come to the larger issues I spoke of. I want you to remove from London; go abroad preferably, until Sarah is safely married. I think Robert treated you shabbily, but I am not going to settle a lump sum on you. I will make you an allowance for life, but,' he regarded her quizzically, 'it ceases if you take up residence in London without my permission.'

'You ought to know better than to try to blackmail me, Louis!'

'Blackmail! Nothing so crude! This is straightforward bribery. With a handsome allowance you can have a very gay time on the continent nowadays, and in a year or so, when all has died down, if you wish, you can come back again. Though I'm afraid there is one more stipulation I must make. You must . . . er . . . regularise your relationship with Matthew Digby for Sarah's sake. To have one's mother living in sin must be a constant source of mortification!'

The countess grinned. 'Going to regularise your relationship with the brunette I saw you with last week, Louis?'

'The cases are entirely different. The lady in question had abandoned the last shreds of her reputation long before I entered her sphere.' He smiled in reply. 'Shall I have a draft agreement drawn up for you?'

'I'm not making any promises,' she said abruptly. 'But have it drawn up by all means. What arrangements will you make for Sarah?'

'I'll take her to Abbotsford and find someone to live with her. The only trouble is that I'm damnably short of relatives. My mother's family are spread about France,

not to mention the fact that I've never met any of 'em.
However, I shall contrive something. You may safely
leave me to take proper care of her.'

'Is that aimed at me?'

'Strangely enough, no,' the earl said, rising to his feet.
'I'll call on you again when we have something more to
discuss.'

'I told you, I'm not making any promises,' she warned.

'If you're thinking to tell me Digby opposes it, don't
try,' the earl said. 'You can wind him round your finger
any time you choose.'

The countess made no reply, and he departed, vaguely
uneasy that she should have proved so malleable.

Some few days later Leonora decided to take a hand in the
affair, but the results of her efforts were not so happy.
With the best of motives, she invited Sarah to go walking
with herself and Maria, and apart from the weather, which
seemed set to rain, the expedition was a success. Sarah got
along famously with Maria; she was pleasant and sweet-
natured, and Leonora felt she would suit Simon very well.

Accordingly, they arranged to visit the shops together,
and change their books at the circulating library, Simon,
much to the astonishment of his sisters, deciding to accompany them.

'But you never would come shopping with us before!'
Maria exclaimed ingenuously.

Simon looked uncomfortable. 'Got one or two things to
purchase myself.'

'Don't tease him,' Leonora recommended. 'What he
means, though he shrinks from putting it into words, is

that our claims he can cheerfully ignore, but Sarah is an entirely different matter. And, after all, he may carry our parcels.'

'I will not!' Simon said, revolted.

'You may see how he behaves in the circle of his family,' Leonora told Sarah. 'If that isn't sufficient to put you off, you must be a sad case.'

Sarah merely gazed worshipfully into his face, and shrugging expressively, Leonora led the way at a brisk pace.

He conducted himself quite creditably in Hookham's, reaching books down for them, and giving his opinion of their choice, but when they came to the shopping he showed a tendency to lag behind.

'It's of no use to pretend you're not with us,' Leonora said. 'You elected to come, and accompany us you shall until the bitter end. Sarah, speak to him! Mama always said it was of the greatest importance to start as you mean to go on. Let him slide out of these little things now, and there will be no controlling him later!'

Sarah looked confused, and Simon cast Leonora a glance of loathing, but obediently quickened his pace.

'What he's really afraid of,' Leonora continued chattily, 'is that some of his fine, roistering friends will see him positively engulfed by petticoats. His image will suffer!'

'One thing I will say for Maria,' Simon said, goaded beyond endurance. 'She ain't got your tongue!' He drew level with them but was afflicted with cowardice when he found they had stopped to look in a milliner's. Retreating a few steps, he pretended to be absorbed in the wares displayed in a silversmith's, contriving to keep them under his eye at the same time.

Leonora and Maria eventually backed off from their study of hats, and were waiting for Sarah when Mrs. Rochford and the Countess Lieven, accompanied by a faintly uncomfortable Mr. Rochford, hove into view. The girls dropped demure curtsies, and Mrs. Rochford swept forward, wreathed in smiles.

'Countess, you must have met Maria and Leonora at Almack's, but did you know Maria was to be my daughter? Delightful girls, are they not?' She extended a hand to each, and the countess gave a tight little smile, and inclined her head in acknowledgement.

Leonora dropped another curtsey, and turned to bring her companion to their notice. But Sarah was shrinking towards the shop window, her reticule clutched tightly in her hand. Turning back, Leonora found the smile had frozen on Mrs. Rochford's face. Her glance flickered over Sarah's distressed countenance, then she smiled brightly at the countess.

'Well, we mustn't hold up the traffic any longer. I daresay I shall see you girls when I call on your mama this afternoon.'

Speechless, Leonora watched them walk away, too furious even to respond to the agonised appeal Mr. Rochford flung back over his shoulder. It was the most cruel and comprehensive snub she had ever seen administered, particularly to a seventeen-year-old girl, unsure of herself in company.

Impulsively, she took Sarah's arm. 'Don't take any notice! Paul said she was bound to bring trouble when she came to town!'

Sarah shook her head, her eyes sparkling with tears. 'You don't understand! I've tried to tell Simon, but he won't believe me!' She looked up as Simon, his face livid, took her other arm protectively.

'That settles it!' he said, with suppressed violence. 'Come on, I'll take you home!'

He marched her off, and Maria, her eyes filled with tears of sympathy, fell into step with Leonora.

'How could anyone be so cruel and heartless?' she said distressfully. 'Poor Sarah!'

'Yes,' Leonora said slowly. 'I begin to see what Mama meant. I thought she was letting herself be ruled by prejudice, but if this is what Simon can expect . . .' Her voice trailed off. 'I suppose I should never have interfered, but Sarah is such a nice girl, and I thought if we could be seen together, and it was known that we accepted her . . . Oh dear! I wonder what Simon will do now?'

Simon had only one thought in mind. He escorted his sisters home, where he was icily polite to his mama, then went out again to restore Sarah to Lady Everard.

'Whatever has put him out so?' Lady Constance said, bewildered. 'I only asked if you'd all had a pleasant morning!'

'Well, we didn't,' Leonora said. She hesitated, then decided that in view of the projected party, Lady Constance would have to be put in possession of the facts.

'We took Sarah with us, and while we were out we met Mrs. Rochford and Countess Lieven, and,' she took a deep breath, 'Mrs. Rochford cut Sarah dead! In front of the countess, and Simon and everyone! I've never felt for anyone so much in my life before. Sarah was terribly upset, and Simon, of course, is furious!'

Lady Constance moaned, and reached for her salts. 'I

told him how it would be! Heaven knows I told him, but he wouldn't listen!'

Leonora said hotly, 'It's completely and utterly unjust! Sarah is not to blame for her mother's faults! She's not much more than a child, and to humiliate her like that in front of other people . . .'

Maria nodded agreement, her eyes filling again as she thought of the scene. 'Mrs. Rochford was quite horrible to her, Mama!'

'Well recollect that she is to be your mother-in-law,' Lady Constance begged. 'If either of you dare to be uncivil to her . . . As though my position wasn't difficult enough already without this being added to it. I shall have to call the whole thing off, though what excuse I can give to Mrs. Rochford I simply do not know.' She sagged in her chair, and reached for her salts again.

Leonora regarded her with genuine pity. 'Perhaps Lord Everard will contrive something,' she said hopefully.

Lady Constance gave vent to another anguished moan. 'How can he? And I wonder what Simon is doing now?'

10

Simon, his original rage having hardened to cold fury, was striding towards Lord Everard's house in Grosvenor Square, his one thought that Sarah should never be made to suffer such mortification again. His mood was not improved when the butler, after one look at his set countenance, said he would discover if his lordship was at home. His tone implied that it was doubtful, and Simon paced the room in angry frustration until the door opened to admit the earl.

He said coolly, 'Good morning.'

'So you are at home!' Simon burst out. 'That fellow was trying to make out you weren't!'

'If you showed him that face I'm not surprised,' the earl said mildly.

Simon stiffened. 'I beg your pardon. Perhaps I should have discovered beforehand whether it was convenient.'

'Simon Revell,' the earl said calmly, 'to the best of my knowledge, I have done nothing to offend you, but if I have, pray sit down and tell me about it. In the meantime, don't be sarcastic!'

'I beg your pardon, sir,' Simon repeated. He remained standing, and swallowed uneasily. There was a long silence while the earl regarded him steadily, then he blurted out, 'I want your permission to marry Sarah, sir!'

'Do you? Do as you're told, and sit down!'

Simon complied, but could not restrain himself from leaning forward eagerly. 'Have I your permission, sir?'

'Not until I know more of this. I knew of your intentions, but something has obviously occurred to bring matters to a head. Let me hear about it!'

'Nothing has occurred!'

The earl stood up, his face implacable. He towered over Simon, still in his chair. For the first time, Simon was aware of the other side to the amiable earl who had taken him to the races. He felt a twinge of what was almost fear, and the earl's next words added to his discomfiture.

'If you knew how much I dislike being taken for a fool,' he was saying wearily. 'You can either show some respect for my intelligence, and tell me the whole, or take yourself off!'

Stumbling and apologising, Simon related the morning's encounter with Mrs. Rochford. He watched the earl's face carefully as he spoke, but it told him nothing. Expressionless, Lord Everard digested the information, then stood up again and rang the bell.

'Well, sir?'

'We'll have a glass of sherry while we discuss it.'

'Can't you give me an answer?'

'When the servant has gone again,' the earl said inexorably.

With almost unbearable impatience Simon waited while the tray was brought in and the earl poured two glasses from the decanter. Handing one over, he said slowly, 'I'm afraid, for the moment, my answer must be no.'

Simon sprang to his feet, slopping the sherry over his fingers. 'But why, sir? What reason . . . ?'

'I have a reason!'

'I don't see why . . .' Simon began furiously.

'Sit down!' The earl's voice was like a whiplash, and in spite of himself Simon sank back. The earl looked down at him with a more kindly expression. 'Let me make it plain that this is by no means my final decision. I said "for the moment." I have not forbidden you to see her, and I have not said that I shall not change my mind. Sarah is only seventeen, and there is plenty of time to think of marriage. I think I should tell you that I am making arrangements for her to stay at Abbotsford, but you will oblige me by keeping this information to yourself for the time being. I cannot tell you the whole at present, and I don't want Sarah to be worried.' He smiled. 'Believe me, I know what I am about. Both your parents have tried to impress the situation upon you, and this morning you had an example for yourself. It would be against the best interests of both of you if I said "Yes" now.'

'But Abbotsford!' Simon said despairingly. 'I shall hardly be able to see her!'

'Nonsense! I shall be going there regularly; you may accompany me on occasions, and it's unlikely that she will lose her heart to someone else while she is away.' He smiled comfortingly. 'The area was not noticeably rich in handsome young bloods when I was last there.' He dropped a hand lightly on Simon's shoulder. 'It would be improper in me to tell you everything, but I repeat, this is the best way.'

'Oh, I know it's Sarah's mother that is the cause of it,' Simon said bitterly.

'I daresay. I am hoping to be able to do something about it, but you will have to be patient. Meanwhile, don't communicate this mood to Sarah. She needs support, not a face of woe!'

'Very well, sir,' Simon said manfully. 'I'll simply tell her that you've said "No" for the present, but you are not against it. I won't mention the other.'

'Good. And don't revert to your old ways because you've suffered disappointment.'

'I won't,' Simon promised. He held out his hand to the earl. 'I won't pretend to be pleased, but I understand.'

Mentally consigning Caroline to the devil, Lord Everard showed him out.

In an attempt to divert Lady Constance's mind, Leonora was boldly confessing that she had consulted Lord Everard on the delicate matter of the party invitations. Any hope, however, that she might be able to gloss over her own unseemly conduct was banished. Lady Constance stared at her, aghast.

'Leonora, you don't mean that you actually asked him? . . . I think I'm going to have a spasm,' she ended feebly.

'Of course you aren't! Only see how much good has come out of it. I defy even the Countess Lieven to ignore Sarah if Lord Everard brings her. And he is bound to make sure that her dress doesn't offend anyone, so there will be no need to worry over that either.'

'You didn't ask him that as well!' Lady Constance cried, starting to her feet.

'No, no, of course I didn't,' Leonora soothed. 'I merely meant that he is very much aware of the awkwardness of the whole situation, and we may rely on him to make sure that everything is as it should be.'

'A man with whom I am barely acquainted,' Lady Constance murmured. 'What he must think of you . . .' She stopped, and a gleam of hope came into her eye. 'Leonora, there isn't any agreement between you? I mean, anything you haven't mentioned to me?'

'Certainly not!' Leonora said, going rigid. 'I've told you before, Mama, that I have not the slightest intention of wedding Lord Everard.' She had a sudden memory of the way his eyes smiled down at her, and her knees turned to water. She sat on the sofa beside Lady Constance and repeated lamely, 'Certainly not!'

Undeterred, Lady Constance went on, 'Even Mrs. Partington quizzed me about it the other day, and she hardly ever goes out into society, so someone must have mentioned it to her.' She stopped, as the reverse view of the matter struck her. 'Leonora, if you don't take care, you will have people saying you are *fast*.'

'Nonsense,' Leonora said defiantly. 'They're far too busy talking about Byron leaving the country!'

'Well, you shouldn't encourage Lord Everard then!'

'I've never given him the least encouragement!' Leonora said indignantly.

Fortunately a diversion occurred as Simon came in. Since he was her chief worry, Lady Constance fell on him, with demands to know where he had been.

Unable to hide his disappointment as well as he might wish, he said, 'If you must know, I've been to see Everard!'

Lady Constance let out a screech. 'Not another one!'

'Why, what's Leonora been up to?' Simon demanded.

'Disgracing me by her want of conduct! I declare I never knew when we came to this house that I should spend the whole of my life in a worry!'

'Why did you go to see Lord Everard?' Leonora interrupted.

'For his permission to marry Sarah, of course!' Simon snapped. 'After this morning I wanted to fix it as soon as possible!'

Almost gibbering with suspense, Lady Constance said, 'But what did he say?'

'He refused!'

The prospect of his mother weeping with undisguised relief proving too much for him, he flung out of the room, Leonora bestowed a quick pat on her parent and followed. She caught up with Simon as he entered their father's study, and closed the door firmly behind her.

'Simon, why did he refuse his consent?'

'Whose side are you on?' Simon demanded belligerently.

'There's no need to take my head off! Yours, of course! I think Sarah is a sweet girl, and so I've told Mama.'

'Well, he hasn't refused altogether, so you may tell her that as well,' he said with satisfaction. 'It should wipe the smile from her face in any event.'

'Oh do stop being so disagreeable, and tell me about it,' Leonora begged.

'There's nothing much to tell. I asked his permission, and he guessed something was up so I had to tell him about this morning.' He flushed slightly as he remembered the earl's tone. 'He said it was no answer to marry her as things stood, but he wasn't refusing altogether. I think he wants to try if he can to re-establish her first. I say, he can be devilish overpowering when he wants to, can't he?'

'Yes,' Leonora said baldly, and trailed away to dwell on the earl's overpowering personality while she rested in preparation for a musical evening, and a late party.

Only Lady Constance and herself were attending the musical evening. Mr. Rochford had cried off in horror, and was taking Maria to visit his mother instead. However, when the appointed time came for him to collect her, it turned out otherwise.

Leonora came down, just as Maria, with an expression of surprise, was taking off her velvet cloak again. Mr. Rochford, somewhat abstracted, bowed to her and nodded to Simon, who glared back with hostility, unfairly holding him responsible for Mrs. Rochford's actions earlier in the day.

'But I thought it was all arranged that we should go,' Maria was saying, puzzled.

Mr. Rochford coughed. 'Best not go tonight. Bit of an atmosphere at home. Had a slight disagreement!'

'Have you had a row with your mother?' Simon demanded, his brow lightening.

'No, no. Well—what I mean is—yes I have!'

'Good for you!' Simon exclaimed, clapping him on the shoulder. 'There I was, thinking you stood it mighty tamely this morning. I take it all back!'

Incensed, Mr. Rochford said, 'I should think so! You'd have had a turn up there in the street with all the fools watching us, I suppose.'

Simon grinned. 'I might have done. I say, best not tell my mother! She'd have hysterics!'

Mr. Rochford eyed him scornfully, and gave an example of his tact when Lady Constance came into the room. She bustled across, exclaiming that she quite thought they'd be gone by now, and asking if she'd mistaken the night, all in one breath.

Mr. Rochford said stolidly that his mother was a trifle indisposed. It was a somewhat free translation of events, as when last seen Mrs. Rochford had been flat on her back, volubly expressing the hope that death would shortly overtake her.

'You will be able to come with us this evening after all,' Lady Constance said brightly.

Harassed, Mr. Rochford said they had already made their apologies.

'Nonsense! Louise Ashford is a very dear friend of mine. I promise you I should be in trouble if she knew I hadn't taken you. They have quite a brilliant pianist there tonight. He's new to England, but I understand he's all the rage on the continent. I daresay it will be very dull, but the *company* will be most interesting.'

Catching his eye, Leonora said in an undervoice, 'Trapped!' and went upstairs to change.

It was to be an elegant evening, and she put on her favourite evening gown with the vandyked flouncing round the hem, and in spite of Lady Constance's oft repeated protests, dressed her hair high on top of her head, allowing the smooth ringlets to fall over one shoulder.

Her mama, popping her head round the door, made no comment on the hair style, but merely said, 'The bronze velvet cloak with that, my love,' and disappeared again.

Mr. Rochford might view the evening with horror, but as an accomplished pianist herself, Leonora was keenly looking forward to it. It proved, however, to be something of a disappointment. Listening with a critical ear, she formed the opinion that the young Italian pianist-composer was not all that his reputation claimed for him. 'In fact,' a voice said in her ear, 'that's the third note he's missed already.'

She jumped, and turned quickly to find Lord Everard bending towards her. 'And how would you know?' she whispered.

'I am familiar with the piece,' he said. 'Come into the other room. I don't think he's worthy of our attention, do you?'

'He's *supposed* to be very good,' she said, placing her fingers on his arm. 'But I didn't know you were musical.'

'I used to play that particular piece when I was younger.'

Leonora was betrayed into an impolite reply. 'You!' she said, in astonishment.

'Spare my blushes! My mother was a noted pianist, and insisted that I learned. It would quite have touched your heart to see me there in my little nankeens, legs dangling from the piano stool!'

Leonora chuckled, then caught herself up. 'Oh dear. My Aunt Margaret is watching us.' She dropped a curtsey, and received a broad smile. 'She's not usually so over-whelming.'

'That is because you are with me,' the earl said, with unbecoming want of modesty. 'I'm quite one of her favourites!' He bowed, and Lady Margaret simpered.

'I wouldn't have believed it!' Leonora said, awed.

'I did imply that you would have a position of the first consequence if you married me!'

Leonora gazed fixedly at the opposite wall, wondering if this last remark was intended to reopen the subject of their marriage. But his tone was bantering, so she said carefully, 'That reminds me. Why have you refused your consent to Simon's marriage with Sarah?'

'I have not refused it,' the earl corrected. 'I have merely forbidden it for the moment. They are both in that happy state where they believe that love can conquer all, and they have to learn that they are wrong. And let me inform you, madam, in case you are about to read me a lecture, that while I am perfectly ready to listen to everyone's advice and opinions, I shall still do what I believe to be right. If the young lovers' hearts are bruised in the process, I'm sorry for it, but in this case, they haven't sufficient worldly sense to judge for themselves.' He regarded her with a lift to his eyebrows. 'You may disagree with me if you wish, but I have eleven more years' experience of the world than you.'

'You wouldn't put any bar in their way,' Leonora insisted. 'Not if it meant their happiness.'

'Oh—oh. Another one who thinks that love is all!'

About to affirm that it was, Leonora suddenly thought of her own case in relation to the earl. 'No,' she said, in a small voice. 'It isn't, of course.'

He glanced down at her quizzically. 'And what hidden meaning is there in that?'

Leonora tossed her head. 'None at all! If you don't mind, I should like to go back and listen to the pianist again.'

'Certainly,' the earl said affably. 'We'll treat ourselves to another glimpse of your Aunt Margaret's dress as we go by. Since you have expressed yourself freely on the subject of my relatives, I think I may be permitted to remark that I find it immodest in the extreme!'

Leonora gave another giggle of laughter. 'Utterly indecent!'

As they listened to the music, she tried to think of any other man of her acquaintance with whom she could converse so freely. Mr. Denston was far too correct ever to notice Lady Margaret's excessive display of bosom, and, of late, Mr. Eccleston appeared to be sending his flowers elsewhere. An impecunious young nobleman was paying her court, but as he was not above eighteen summers, and regarded her in the light of a goddess, she felt a little restricted in his company.

Lord Everard was the only man with whom she could feel completely at ease. The last half hour had been pure enjoyment. She stole a glance sideways at him. He was watching the pianist, apparently with complete concentration, but almost as though he felt her eyes upon him, he turned his head and smiled down at her. The next time marriage was so much as hinted at, Leonora vowed, she would not turn the subject aside.

She came to with a start as the earl nudged her. 'If you are remaining for the next part,' he murmured, 'you stay alone!'

'How ungallant. What is it?'

'A soprano whom I was privileged to hear at the start of the season. She was held to be in very fine voice on that occasion, and it effectively killed any desire to listen to her again in case she should be off her form!'

'You cannot be musical!'

'Quite the contrary! I refuse to have my senses lacerated a second time. Let us go and raise your mama's hopes by mingling in the other room!'

They slipped from their seats, and passed through the arched doorway to where refreshments were being served from a long table at the side of the room. The dishes were interspersed with huge bowls of spring flowers, which charmingly set off the whole. Lord Everard, however, after critically inspecting the fare, said in an undervoice that he wished Louise Ashford would curb her taste for floral decorations at least at the supper table. 'If you have a relish for fragmented fern,' he continued, 'let me recommend the apricot tartlets. They're quite smothered!'

As Leonora choked over the iced confection halfway in her mouth, he observed, 'There is also a sprinkling of something in the lemonade—if only I could remember my botany! The champagne, however, appears to be unadulterated.' He raised an enquiring eyebrow, and Leonora looked dubious.

'I don't know whether I ought. We're going on to a party when we leave here.'

'One glass should hardly cause you to violate the social codes, but don't if you're doubtful.'

'I can always drink lemonade at the Hadlingtons'.'

He passed her a glass across and raised his own. 'Your health, ma'am. Did I mention that you are in very good looks tonight? You should always wear your hair like that.'

It was the first straightforward compliment he had ever paid her, and she was cast into some confusion. She murmured something about it making her over tall.

'Not for me,' the earl said, measuring her with his eye.

'You are not the only man I am like to stand beside,' Leonora returned with spirit.

'No,' the earl admitted. 'But you realise, of course, that half the people in this room will now be expecting to hear the news of our betrothal!'

Leonora took a deep breath, and prepared to hint that her sentiments might have undergone a change. Unfortunately, the right words would not immediately come to mind, and in searching for a phrase of sufficient delicacy, she hesitated too long. Lady Constance was at her elbow, saying it was time for them to leave, Mr. Rochford converged on them, and the earl was bowing over her hand.

She could have sworn with vexation, but meeting his eyes, she had the impression that he had divined her thoughts. Which would have been all to the good, she thought crossly, if he had not also conveyed that he was secretly laughing at her.

The earl, in fact, was highly amused, but he was not the man to pander to the contrariness of his beloved. By now, he was in no doubt of her feelings for him. They had the ease of friendship, as well as the warmer feelings he considered necessary for marriage. His lips twitched when he recalled how easily he could reduce her to laughter or rage with a few well chosen words. His loved one was over impulsive, and while he would not change her, she should learn that the Earl of Everard was not to be led by the nose like the accommodating Mr. Denston.

He emptied his glass, and sought out his hostess to take his leave and compliment her on the quality of the entertainment, and interestedly observed by every pair of eyes in the room, departed. It was noted by all that he had not stayed above five minutes after the departure of Miss Revell, and opinion was divided fairly equally between those who thought they made a pleasing couple, and the hopeful mothers and daughters who considered it a crying shame that one of the season's biggest catches seemed likely to fall to an upstart from the country.

In a mood of recklessness engendered by a third glass of champagne, the upstart was going back over the evening's conversation, and mentally chiding herself for the opportunities she had missed. While the effects of the champagne lasted, she even considered writing to him, but in the cold light of day her resolve vanished. Though he had made frequent references to marriage, she was bound to admit that they had been of a somewhat jocular nature. He had never, in so many words, actually repeated his offer, and she was not going to fling herself at any man's head. If only the wretched man would ask her a second time!

Like Catherine Harford before her, she began scanning every room as she entered, and felt her heart sink each time he was not there. At the end of the week, she was beginning to despair. If the earl's feelings were as strong as she believed, he would surely not let seven days go by without contacting her.

Did she but know it, the earl felt the time lapse as keenly as she. Each morning he planned to call on her, but each morning he found himself with so little time that he put off his visit until the following day in the hope that he might be with her longer.

For this, the Countess of Everard was responsible. The earl had induced his normally longwinded lawyers to draw up the agreement, and Caroline had put her signature to it. Once this was done, she wanted to be away, and the earl felt himself obliged to assist her. The countess stated flatly that since she was not moving from her own choice, he could make himself responsible for everything it entailed, including the re-letting of the house, and the storing of all the furniture that was her own. Everything she was to take with her was stowed into trunks and boxes to await the carrier, and he arranged for her funds to be transferred and paid into a Paris bank.

Throughout all this, Sarah remained strangely listless. Perturbed, the earl watched her keenly, and several times asked her if she was unhappy at the thought of removing to Abbotsford. Sarah shook her head. Her mother, she said, had explained that it was necessary, and though she was naturally a little nervous, she was quite prepared.

'It won't be for ever you know,' the earl said with a smile, 'and I shall bring Simon to see you I promise.'

Her eyes filled with tears, and she looked away quickly, leaving the earl more troubled than ever, but he came to the conclusion that it was a natural reaction in a girl of only seventeen. However lacking the countess might be as a parent, Sarah had never been parted from her before, and to be separated from both her and Simon, and, at the same time, to be sent to a strange home, must be daunting.

He was also a little disturbed by the countess's attitude. She was a woman who disliked having her hand forced, and he had expected more opposition when the time actually came. Her too ready acquiescence made him uneasy.

But the main problem arising out of her sudden desire to be gone, was finding someone suitable to live with Sarah. At such short notice, he was forced to fall back on the mistreated cousin Henrietta, who was living with relatives in Worcestershire. Knowing full well that an entreaty

through the mails would meet with a flat refusal, the earl
set out to try the effects of his personal charm.

Cousin Henrietta agreed, though reluctantly, and after
arranging for the transport of herself and the numerous
items she considered necessary to her comfort, the earl set
out for London again.

Normally, he was a great admirer of the rolling hills of
Worcestershire, and this time of year, just breaking into
the green of spring, they were particularly beautiful, but
on this occasion he was more concerned with the deplorable state of the roads and the using of his time. Cousin
Henrietta, he knew, was not the proper answer. She was a
suitable, if unexciting, companion, but she could not give
Sarah standing. Something else must be thought of.

He had the time in which to think, for the return journey took an extra day. The rain-swollen river carried away
a bridge, and in casting about for another place to cross,
he lost the main post road. Nursing his tired team through
the mud, the earl was inclined to call down curses on the
heads of all women, Caroline in particular, and the posting
house which he eventually honoured with his custom was
not of the style he favoured.

After eating an indifferent dinner, he inspected the
sheets, and decided to spend the night on top of the cov-
ers, which, while it saved him from the previous occu-
pant's dirt, was not conducive to either warmth or comfort.

By the time the birds set up their dawn chorus, he was
heartily sick of his couch, and sallied forth to do battle
with the landlord over the matter of his breakfast. He discovered that the class of customer the inn normally ca-
tered for, set a much lower standard on their fare than he

did himself, and went into the yard to study with a fascinated eye the team that was to take him on to the next stage.

Never before had he seen so many splints and spavins and capped hocks assembled together, and after closing his eyes in disbelief, he enquired, in failing tones, whether the inn could furnish him with a different team.

The postboy, who disdained wearing a smock over his uniform, or indeed, as far as the earl could see, disdained any uniform at all, said the other team was out, and he wouldn't like to try driving the pairs, as he doubted whether they would go together.

Resignedly, the earl begged him not to try if he was in any doubt at all, and prayed that the stage would be a short one.

Midway through the third morning, he arrived back at the town house, tired, heartily sick of hired horses, and for one of his equable temperament, unusually ruffled.

Tossing down his driving coat, he replied briefly to the footman who expressed the hope that he had had a pleasant journey, and was gathering up the collection of correspondence, when the butler cleared his throat.

He glanced up with a slight frown. At the back of his mind was a nagging certainty that there was something he had missed in this affair of the removal of the countess; it eddied back and forth, defying his efforts to pin it down.

Abruptly, he said, 'Well?'

'There is someone to see you, my lord.' The butler cleared his throat again. 'A young lady! I put her in the Blue Saloon.'

'Who is it?'

'She would not give a name, my lord!'

With an exclamation, the earl threw the letters down again, and crossed the hall. In the doorway, he stopped, thunderstruck, as he saw who awaited him.

'And just what are you doing here?' he said grimly.

Facing him with an expression as set as his own, Leonora said, 'I came to see you!'

'Obviously, madam, but you can just turn yourself about and go right back again. What do you think you are doing, coming here, and alone as far as I can make out?'

'I could think of nowhere else I could freely express my opinion of you!'

'Leonora,' the earl said wearily, 'let us have no riddles. What is this about?'

'What is it about?' Leonora repeated furiously. 'You pretend you don't know! What have you done with Sarah?'

In the earl's mind something clicked into place. It struck him now that while he had made almost every other arrangement for Caroline, she had not asked him to book her passage, and she had already possessed a passport.

'Are you trying to make me believe that you don't know where she is?' Leonora demanded.

'I know where she is well enough,' the earl said shortly. And there she could stay for the time being, he thought, remembering the discomforts of his now fruitless journey into Worcestershire. He was also annoyed that Leonora could so readily believe him to be the villain of the plot. 'What does Simon have to say?'

Leonora's lip quivered. 'He hasn't been home since yesterday morning!'

'Well he's had four days besides in which to express an opinion, and if his only reaction when he suffers a setback, is to go off and get himself drunk, then it merely confirms my belief that they are neither of them fit for marriage,' the earl said blightingly.

'How do you know what he is doing?' Leonora flashed.

'I'll lay you a hundred to one! Now will you oblige me by returning home? You had no business coming here in the first place, as you very well know. How did you get here, by the way?'

'I walked,' Leonora said sullenly.

'Unattended!' He made it sound like the grossest impropriety, and Leonora's lower lip thrust out further. 'It will probably be less singular if I escort you back. Don't trouble to tell me you don't wish me to!'

Leonora shut her mouth with a snap, and kept it closed until she was on her own doorstep, where she thanked him icily for his escort. Knowing better than to offer his hand, the earl bowed in return, and frowning, started back down the street.

For the first time he was irritated with Leonora, and he cherished thoughts of wringing Sarah's neck when he should catch up with her. For a moment he considered whether he should set out again immediately, but he had his fill of travel in the last few days. He had already expended enough energy on Sarah's behalf. Whatever the reason for her flight, it could wait.

11

Entering the hall, Leonora walked straight into the arms of Lady Constance. She stepped back guiltily, and Lady Constance fell on her.

'Where have you been, you dreadful girl? First it is Simon, then you! When Collins said you had gone out alone I . . .'

'Is Simon back?' Leonora interrupted.

'Yes. But that is neither here nor there. Don't think to turn me aside! You went out alone, and without a word to anyone, and as your mother, I demand to know where you have been!'

'I went to see Lord Everard!'

Lady Constance screamed, and collapsed against the hall table. 'It was a mistake! A mistake ever to come here! We should have stayed at Revell House, and at least I should have escaped seeing us all brought to ruin! My son brought home senseless, and my daughter disgraced in the eyes of the world!'

Alarmed, Leonora said quickly, 'Has Simon met with an accident?'

'No,' Lady Constance sobbed. 'He was brought home disgustingly inebriated by a man who found him in some ow tavern, and discovered his card upon him. Sarah is a nice enough girl, but I must admit I was thankful to find she had gone. At least, I should have been,' she amended, 'if only Simon had taken it sensibly. She cannot really have cared for him to go off like that, for the house is closed and all the servants dismissed, so she cannot intend coming back. He will not have it that she has gone of her own free will, and holds that Lord Everard must be responsible.' Returning to the thread of her discourse, she said, 'Why did you go to see Lord Everard?'

'To find out where Sarah is, of course. And he does know though he wouldn't say! We knew he must, of course. For them both to be gone on the same day couldn't be coincidence!'

'Well I'm sure it's nothing to me now,' Lady Constance said fretfully. 'If any one of us receives vouchers for Almack's again, it will be a miracle. To go alone to a gentleman's establishment! And in Grosvenor Square, above all places, where anyone may see you go in and out!'

'I was with him no more than five minutes,' Leonora said defensively.

'But you were gone from here above an hour!'

'He didn't arrive home until just before I left.'

'People who saw you enter and leave are not to know that,' Lady Constance pointed out. 'And I'm sure one may be ruined just as effectively in half the time. We are due at Lady Durrell's tonight,' she ended despairingly, 'and she lives on the opposite side of the square. I only hope she may not have been watching through her windows!'

'I daresay we shall find out if she was! Where is Simon?'

Lady Constance flung up her hands. 'Still senseless on his bed for all I know!'

'Then he won't be going tonight in any event,' Leonora commented fatalistically.

The reaction to her brief exchange with the earl set in, and she felt so low that evening that she nearly cried off herself. Lady Constance, however, was almost tearfully insistent that she must put in an appearance, so she tried to put a bright face on it.

Since it no longer mattered what Lord Everard thought of her, she dressed her hair in a different way, and the result was not happy. Without the lift which the extra height gave, her face lost some of its vivaciousness. Or perhaps, Leonora thought drearily, it was simply that she was not feeling vivacious. No doubt this awful feeling of depression would pass, but it seemed, at the moment, that life held nothing to look forward to, and she longed to indulge her misery behind the curtains of her bed.

Emerging from her room, she knew she still looked hagged, and it was of no help when Lady Constance commented on it, adding that she looked as though she hadn't been to bed for a week.

'I feel as though I hadn't! How long must we stay tonight?' Lady Constance's face fell, and she said quickly, 'Never mind. I expect I shall brighten up once we are there.'

Determinedly, she smiled her way through the first part of the evening, even pointing out maliciously to Lady Constance that the news of her loose behaviour did not appear to have spread abroad, and she was an interested observer to the heated quarrel which broke out between Catherine Harford and Sir Mark Finchley in the middle of the ballroom floor.

Which was an idiotic place to conduct it, she whispered
to her mama, for how could one retain one's line of argument when constantly separated by other couples. Catherine flounced angrily off the floor at the end of the dance,
and Leonora watched with simple enjoyment as Sir Mark
scurried after her, his rather short legs almost trotting to
keep up, his face red with suppressed temper.

About to drop an acid comment into Lady Constance's
ear, she perceived Lord Everard a few feet distant, and
her evening was spoiled. She felt her own face become
frosty as he caught her eye, and regretted it immediately.
He had taken a few steps towards her, but now he bowed
and turned away again.

Watching him as he walked away, she had almost decided that whatever he had done, it didn't matter if only
he would smile at her again, when she saw Catherine Harford tilt a provocative glance at him from under her
lashes. Stiffening indignantly, Leonora saw him alter
course like a moth to a candle, and bow over her hand
with an extravagant flourish. Sir Mark was squaring up
like a gamecock, and if it had been any other man than the
earl involved in the comedy, Leonora would have laughed
aloud at the way he removed her from under Sir Mark's
nose. Obviously the quarrel was still in progress from the
triumphant glance Catherine threw back over her
shoulder, and it re-commenced the moment the earl
brought her back from their waltz. Their voices began to
be raised above their fellows, and people turned to look at
them. Catherine's shrill tones penetrated above the music,
and Sir Mark lost his temper and shouted back.

All in all, it was a most entertaining spectacle, and Lord
Everard, instead of decently removing himself, stayed to

enjoy it. Whatever had been the original cause of disharmony, it soon became apparent the earl was the backbone of contention between them. His lips turned up with amusement as his name was brought more and more frequently into their bickering, and at one point, he was unwise enough to murmur 'Bravo' in encouragement.

Sir Mark whirled round on him, his face suffused with rage and the wine he had been drinking all evening. It was one of those rare moments of quiet to be found at a noisy gathering. The orchestra were silent, selecting their music for the next piece, and the people nearby had abandoned conversation and were unashamedly listening. Into the hush, Sir Mark's words fell like a thunderbolt.

'You!' he snarled. 'You're the cause of this, but by God you'll pay for it. I've stood enough!' His voice rose higher on a slightly hysterical note. 'I'll tell everyone what I know! Everyone here tonight!'

He swung round the circle of watchers, and Leonora's throat tightened with fear, anticipating what was to come.

'Lord Everard,' Sir Mark sneered. 'The great Lord Everard! You've all fawned over him—crawled to him! Invited him into your homes!' His eyes rested on the Hon. Mrs. Harford, open-mouthed with astonishment. 'Prayed he'd notice your daughters! Shall I tell you who he is? Shall I tell you how he's hoodwinked you all?" He paused, and the earl's voice cut in like a knife.

'That's enough, Finchley!'

'No it isn't,' Sir Mark said thickly. 'I'm going to tell them—all of them!' Raising his voice, he shouted, 'He's the Black Gentleman! A common highwayman! Don't you believe me? He held me up last year, and I shot him!'

There was a hiss of indrawn breath from those around,

and Sir Mark laughed triumphantly. 'Ask him to show you the scar on his arm! Ask him if he dares!'

There was a stunned silence, and Leonora heard her own voice say, clearly and steadily, 'Nonsense!'

Sir Mark stared at her, stupefied. It was patently obvious that she was of so little moment to him that he had completely forgotten her presence on that night. She walked forward calmly.

'I was with Sir Mark when he shot the highwayman, and it certainly was not Lord Everard. The whole idea is utterly preposterous!'

'But you spoke to him!' Sir Mark exclaimed. 'You know . . .'

'Certainly I spoke to him,' Leonora interrupted coldly. 'He was right up to the window of my coach, and I had an excellent view of him. I repeat, I am completely positive that it was not Lord Everard. I cannot imagine why Sir Mark has trumped up this tale, unless . . .' She allowed her eyes to rest for a moment on Catherine Harford, and her voice trailed away.

Sir Mark seemed to shrink. She knew he made some sort of apology to the earl, but people were pressing round her with questions, and the rest of it was lost to her. An excitable young woman was declaring that she would have died of fright if such a thing had happened to her; another was wanting an exact description of the Black Gentleman. Lady Constance's alarmed face was watching her from the fringe of the crowd, mouth agape.

She said, 'Excuse me,' and began to push her way out; their hostess signed to the orchestra to strike up the next dance, and she was alone at the side of the room. Her hands and knees were trembling, and she sat down and pretended to be searching in her reticule, so that she didn't see the earl until he was standing above her. She gave a small gasp.

He said simply, 'Thank you, Leonora.'

Perversely, she wanted to cry, then anger welled up in her. As cuttingly as she could, she said, 'Now that your last fear is removed, you may marry your precious Catherine Harford in peace!'

For a moment, the earl stood silent, an arrested expression in his eyes, then he gave a small bow and turned on his heel. Leonora saw him make his way towards Lady Durrell and exchange a few words with her, then he was gone.

Somehow she survived the rest of the evening. Lady Constance inclined at first to think that after making such a prominent figure of herself, her best course would be to fade quietly away, changed her mind, and said Leonora had done quite right to defend the earl against Sir Mark's scurrilous aspersions.

She emerged, flushed and exhilarated, from a bout with a severe and elderly matron, who had ventured a criticism of her daughter's forwardness, and said Leonora must by no means go home. If there were any more such as Flora Hettrick who had anything to say, she would prefer to deal with them there and then. She quartered the ballroom with an air of pugnacity, a little disappointed to find that Sir Mark had also gone, and was moved to compliment Leonora on her rare foresight in turning him down.

Uneasily aware that she had served Sir Mark a turn he did not deserve, Leonora remained silent, and prayed that their departure would not be long distant. It was gone two o'clock however, before Lady Constance decided there was no one else against whom she would be called upon to defend her daughter's conduct, and worn out with her mixture of emotions, Leonora was able to fall into her bed.

After a miserable night, she came down next morning in an alarmingly militant mood. Lady Constance, after one look at her face, confined herself to trivialities, but Simon, combining sheepishness with the outward aspect of a broken heart, launched into a bitter diatribe against the earl. Banging the coffee pot down with a force that rattled the cups on the table, Leonora leapt to her feet and informed them that if anyone again mentioned Lord Everard in her presence, she would not be responsible for the consequences.

She then ordered her grey to be saddled, and defiantly dispensing with the groom, disappeared in the direction of the park and was gone the whole morning.

Simon said everyone in the house seemed to have run mad, and went off to call on the earl, where the butler, with some satisfaction, once more informed him that his lordship was from home. Fuming with frustration on the step, Simon asked when he would be back.

'As to that, sir, I could not say. Except that his lordship has taken the big travelling carriage, so I should judge it to be a journey of some distance.'

There was nothing to do but return home. The aftermath of the previous day's potations still hanging heavy on him, he winced at the idea of any convivial gathering, and with Sarah gone, he did not have the heart to ride alone.

He contemplated returning to her house to try again if he could discover any lead to her whereabouts, but the house was shut up and none of the neighbours could help, and he already knew from his enquiries that she had not gone to Abbotsford. That suggestion, no doubt, had merely been a red herring to blind him to the earl's real intentions. What these could be he had no very clear idea, but his being from home on the morning Sarah disappeared argued complicity in the matter.

He occupied himself on the way by picturing his heroic rescue of Sarah from various unpleasant predicaments, but he was not by nature particularly melodramatic, and he failed even to convince himself. Certainly he could not imagine himself wreaking vengeance on the earl. Lord Everard was a large, and extremely powerfully built man, and physical violence was out of the question, as were swords. Not only were they out of fashion, but with the earl's tremendous reach, Simon suspected that he would be skewered like a muffin on a toasting fork, and of what use would he be to Sarah dead?

When he did reach home, he relieved his feelings by quarrelling royally with the entirely innocent Maria, and decided that all human relationships were hollow. The result of this, was that without any consultation with Lady Constance, he sallied forth and bought himself a large red setter, the companionship of dumb animals being superior to that of mankind.

Lady Constance, having already had complaints of his conduct from a tearful Maria, discovered the animal when she went to remonstrate with him. It was a boisterous, unrestrained creature, in the latter stages of puppyhood, and in the excitement of its new surroundings, desecrated the blue velvet curtains of the study before her very eyes. She succumbed to mild hysterics on being informed that it was to be a permanent feature of the house, and tottered away to add yet another footnote to her letter to Mr. Revell.

This epistle had begun the previous week when she had entertained high hopes of Leonora and Lord Everard, and progressed through his unaccountable absence and Sarah's disappearance, to Simon's fall from grace.

There were hurried additions to cover Leonora's shocking want of conduct in calling at the earl's home, and the scene at the Durrell's ball, and finally, the inclusion into the household by Simon of a large dog, more fit for a country estate, which had already demonstrated its lamentable lack of training in the study.

Leonora's entrance, in the middle of the last paragraph, brought forth in a flood the salient points of this letter, and quite forgetting the unfortunate stir at the breakfast table, Lady Constance made a reference to the earl. The effect was immediate. Leonora delivered herself of her opinion of the earl and all he stood for, and what would be his fate if it was left to her.

She then announced her determination to wed Mr. Denston. She had met him in the park. He was most truly the gentleman, and he would be waiting on Mr. Revell as soon as he should come to town.

Her salts clutched in her left hand, Lady Constance added another footnote to the effect that Leonora had gone stark raving mad, but not to trouble himself by coming up to London because it was all of a piece with the rest of the household, and no doubt he would become used to it.

Upon receipt of this distracted communication, Mr. Revell once more abandoned his estates. Dearly though he loved his Constance, he recognised that she was not the woman to deal with emergencies where Leonora and his son were concerned.

Unravelling, not without difficulty, the intricacies of her story, he demanded a bottle of wine, and had recourse to his snuff while he considered it. Lady Constance, hopefully awaiting his verdict, was not much comforted when he said that since the earl had always struck him as a sensible man of more than ordinary intelligence, he could only suppose that it must be Leonora and Simon who were at fault. He then asked if Simon had called at the earl's house that day.

'Called today!' Lady Constance echoed. 'I'm surprised he doesn't camp upon his doorstep!'

'Well nothing can be done until Lord Everard returns,' Mr. Revell said calmly. 'But in the meantime, I'll just have a few words with Simon.'

The recipient of his few words emerged chastened some half hour later. Mr. Revell, by the application of a little common sense, had reduced his wild conclusions to the level of a farce.

Why, asked Mr. Revell, should Lord Everard, who had shown himself remarkably open and forbearing in his last interview with Simon, suddenly, and for no apparent reason, spirit Sarah away?

Simon muttered that he didn't know. No doubt he had a reason, and he would like to know where he was now.

'I should imagine,' Mr. Revell said, dusting himself with snuff, 'that he has gone in search of his ward, for whom, let me remind you, he is legally responsible!' He regarded his son with some severity. 'And when he returns, I suggest you treat him with the courtesy to which he is entitled.'

Nodding dismissal, he sent for Leonora, and settled back with his feet on the hearth. The female mind, particularly Leonora's, he found more difficult to understand.

She came in, still in her mood of belligerence. He indicated the chair opposite, and waited until she was seated, then said, 'I hear you intend to marry young Denston.' She nodded, and he continued, 'Your mother had hopes that there might be something between you and Lord Everard.'

Leonora lifted her chin. 'Mama exaggerates it!'

'Really,' Mr. Revell said interestedly. 'Then explain this!' Taking her letter to the earl from his pocket, he held it out. 'Prevarication will not serve, my child. You accepted him then changed your mind.'

Leonora flushed a quick scarlet, and sat biting her lip. For a moment, she considered telling him the whole; it would be a relief to discuss it with someone, and listen to their advice, but keeping the earl's secret had become second nature. She said indifferently, 'I am persuaded he would have lived to regret it. It was the day after Catherine Harford settled for Mark Finchley.'

'Leonora,' Mr. Revell said patiently, 'are you seriously telling me that you believe Lord Everard to be the kind of man who would propose in a fit of pique?'

'Oh he likes me well enough, but marriage never entered his head until she turned him down.'

'Your mother tells me there was some commotion connected with Everard at a ball the other night,' Mr. Revell said carefully, 'and that you came to his defence.' He raised his eyebrows on a query, and Leonora stared back defiantly.

'I suppose I may keep my sense of justice!'

'There's more to it than that, my child. Don't think to pull the wool over my eyes. I don't know what game you're playing, but Everard isn't the man to be trifled with!'

'Nor am I to be trifled with!'

'Well I'll do what I can for you,' Mr. Revell sighed. 'When Denston applies to me I shall refuse my consent, and let's hope you come to your senses before you come of age!'

Leonora left the room on a flounce that carried her halfway up the stairs, deeply grieved that her father, whom she had always regarded as an understanding man, should have joined the enemy camp.

Excusing himself from dinner on the grounds that she was not hungry, and a card party because of a headache, she took a book, and Simon's dog for company, and shut herself in the study.

It was gone nine o'clock when the porter answered the front door to find Lord Everard and his ward upon the step. He asked for Lady Constance, and doubtfully, the servant showed him into the hall. Her ladyship, he knew, was only home because of the unfortunate circumstance of a new pair of slippers which had caused her agony during the first part of the evening, and she had merely popped in to change them before carrying on to another engagement.

She came down the stairs to discover the earl still waiting there, and uttered a sharp reproof to the porter.

'It's no fault of his, Lady Constance,' the earl said, with a slight smile. 'I am in all my dirt, and would not go in.'

She saw that the skirts of his driving coat were dirty and mud splashed, and his normally brilliant hessians caked about the heels. When he reached out a hand to take hers, he withdrew it with a grimace.

'You see, ma'am, I warned you!'

'Oh nonsense,' Lady Constance said briskly. 'Come in and I'll get you some refreshment. You look tired to death!'

He shook his head. 'No, I thank you, though if I could solicit your kindness on behalf of my ward . . .'

'Is Sarah here?' Lady Constance said, astonished. 'But I thought . . .'

'I've brought her back, ma'am, which is why I am here. If you could give her a bed for tonight, I shall be eternally grateful to you. She has no maid with her, so I do not care to put her into an hotel, particularly at this hour, and she is too unwell to travel any further. I shall relieve you of her in the morning.'

'Oh, poor child!' Lady Constance exclaimed. 'Of course she must stay. Where have they put her? In the front saloon? Never mind your dirt and come in with me.'

She led the way, and smiling to himself, the earl followed.

Sarah was crouched by the fire, a small woebegone figure, with strands of pale hair escaping down her white face. Her expression told that she was by no means sure of her welcome, and touched Lady Constance as nothing else could have done.

'I'm sorry, ma'am,' she faltered. 'You are dressed to go out. Lord Everard brought me here because travel upsets me, but . . .'

She stopped, smothered, as Lady Constance enveloped her in a hug.

'It's of no moment, child, they won't miss us, and I don't know what Lord Everard was about to keep you travelling so late!' She glared accusingly at the earl, who smiled, well pleased with her change of attitude.

'One of the horses went lame miles from anywhere and delayed us. At the time, it seemed better to come straight on than to put up at a strange inn. As I said, Sarah has no maid with her.'

'Well she must have something to eat, and then go straight to bed,' Lady Constance said determinedly. 'Come, you haven't even taken off your cloak.'

'She wouldn't take it off before,' the earl said, unable to resist temptation.

Lady Constance looked a trifle confused, but then the door opened to admit Simon. 'Collins told me Sarah . . .' he began, then saw her by the fire. They rushed into each other's arms, while the earl looked on benignly. He glanced down at Lady Constance, who could not prevent a shade of anxiety from crossing her face.

'It will be all right, ma'am, I promise you. I will give you a full explanation presently, but I should like to see Leonora first. Is she at home?'

'Leonora!' she said, coming to with a start. 'Yes, she is in. She stayed home because she has the migraine, but . . .' She looked up at the earl doubtfully.

'It's extremely urgent. If I could just have a few words with her in private.'

'Well I'll tell her but you know what she is,' Lady Constance said, Leonora's unflattering descriptions still sharp in her memory. 'You had best come into the library.'

What arts were employed, the earl never knew, but

presently she came down. She stood by the door, refusing to come any further into the room, and said stonily, 'What do you want?'

The earl smiled tiredly. 'To quote you on our first meeting, nothing so much as my bed. You see I do remember.'

'I am not interested in your recollections, sir,' Leonora returned, her expression unchanging.

He made a wry face. 'Unpromising! Do you mind if I sit down? It seems to have been a very long day.' He let himself down into one of the easy chairs, and straightened his right leg with a wince.

'What's the matter?' Leonora asked, in slightly altered tones.

'One of the wheelers kicked me when I was unhitching it in the dark. Careless of me.'

For the first time Leonora noticed the earl's travel-stained appearance. 'What on earth were you doing to be travelling in the dark?'

'Covering the distance home in as short a time as possible—to ask you again to marry me.'

'I wouldn't marry you . . .'

'Leonora,' the earl interrupted wearily, 'I have spent an extremely tiring and tedious six days on your behalf. I have travelled backwards and forwards across France like a tennis ball. I have endured a scene with my cousin Caroline which some would describe as shattering, and I have been shut up in a coach with a weeping female, who, admittedly through no fault of her own, does not travel well. You will marry me whether you like it or not!'

'What weeping female?' Leonora said, fastening on to the one item.

'Sarah. I have removed her from Caroline's care once

and for all, and restored her to your mother. The only way out of this tangle, is to place her under the chaperonage of some respectable female, until her character is re-established, and you, my love, are going to be that female. We are going to be married and take Sarah to live with us, and at the end of the year, you will present her to society, and she may announce her betrothal to your brother. If she is sponsored by the decorous Lady Everard there will be no difficulty. Though,' he grinned maliciously, 'you will have to mend your ways!'

'You want to marry me to provide a chaperone for Sarah,' Leonora said in a small voice.

'No, my love,' the earl returned. 'I have always wanted to marry you, as you very well know, but for an intelligent young woman you get some very hare-brained notions into your head. Did you really think I asked you because I was afraid of what you might disclose?'

Leonora found her knees had suddenly gone weak, and sat down on the chair opposite. Refusing to meet his eyes, she said, 'But it all fitted together so well. The first time we met, you asked me if I had ever mentioned it to Sir Mark, and I was so confused, I don't know what I said in reply. I know I didn't give you a proper answer, and then I wouldn't say how I had recognised you because I was offended.'

'Contrary to the last,' the earl commented. 'What other devious little thoughts did you have?' His eyes gleamed. 'Tell me about the morning after that very interesting ball at Lady Netherby's.'

'No,' Leonora said, flushing.

'I could tell you. When the fair Catherine was apparently lost to me, you thought I had decided that the best thing

would be to marry you in case you should back up Finchley's story. What a pretty character you must think me!'

'I *wanted* to marry you,' Leonora said desperately, 'but
I kept telling myself I should be a fool if I did.'

'My love,' the earl said, getting to his feet and folding
her in his arms, 'you are a fool!'

Some time later, Leonora raised her head and said,
'There is something I ought to tell you.'

'Lancashire mills!'

'How did you know?'

'Paul told me. He also knows about my own reprehensible past. He played a very prominent part in my return.'

'I do think you might have told me!'

'There has been a want of openness all around. Now be
quiet!'

Ignoring him, Leonora said, 'Poor Sarah! How is she?'

'Much recovered by now I imagine. She is spending the
night here, and when I last saw her she was expressing her
happiness at being reunited with Simon. I own that when
she said travel made her unwell, I didn't realise quite what
she meant by it!'

'Then why did you drag her all that way tonight?'

'Because I came to the conclusion that if she was going
to be sick anyway, it might just as well be tonight as tomorrow,' the earl said brutally.

'How heartless!'

'By no means,' he said firmly. He pulled her across to
the sofa and settled her in the circle of his arm. 'I could
see no point in prolonging the agony!'

Leonora laid her head against his coat. 'You smell of
horses. Why did Sarah go off like that if you weren't responsible?'

'Because, she says, she realised the morning Mrs. Rochford refused to recognise her, that she would be doing Simon no good if she married him. A thing I did my best to impress upon both of them.' He flattened a dusky curl that was tickling his nose. 'I've a deal of wisdom to impart if only people would listen to me. I had already prevailed upon Caroline to make her home temporarily on the continent, and dear Sarah resolved to make a martyr of herself and part from Simon For Ever, so she persuaded Caroline to take her with her. I understand that she put all this in a very affecting letter which Simon will probably receive tomorrow. She cried over me all the way here, convinced that she was bringing your wretched brother to utter ruin.' He sighed. 'If only they would take my advice and leave things to me.'

'Do you mean you've left that poor girl still not knowing what is going to happen to her?' Leonora said indignantly.

Eyes glinting, the earl said, 'And what would you have had me tell her? You have not been precisely encouraging recently.'

Leonora admitted it. 'But there is no reason why we shouldn't tell her now.'

'No reason at all,' the earl said, kissing the top of her head. 'And I am immensely looking forward to telling your mother. I think I may confidently predict that it will make her year!'